"We had a deal, remember?

"I help you out, and you let me be there when my brother is arrested."

Dominic narrowed his eyes. "The deal was, you help, and I do my best to keep Michael alive. That's all there was to it. It's not safe for you to be involved with the arrest."

Jessica stiffened her spine and squared her shoulders. "If I want to be target practice for the bad guys, that's my business, not yours. Look, *Mr. U.S. Deputy Marshal.* Michael trusts me. If I'm there, maybe he'll turn himself in without a fight."

"And maybe he won't. Until I know you're safe, you're not leaving the marshals' custody."

"Oh, yes, I am!" She glared at him and headed for the door, but Dominic wasn't moving. He was big and strong and looked absolutely magnificent as he blocked the door. A hint of attraction swept over her, and she gritted her teeth.

The last thing she wanted was to be attracted to this tall, bullheaded deputy.

KATHLEEN TAILER

is an attorney who works for the Supreme Court of Florida in the Office of the State Courts Administrator where she works on programs that are designed to enhance and improve dependency courts throughout the state. She previously worked for the Florida Department of Children and Families handling child abuse cases both as a line attorney, and in the DCF General Counsel's Office. She and her husband have eight children, five of whom they adopted. When not in the office, Kathleen spends most of her time cheering for her kids at different events or spending quiet time (hah!) at home. Kathleen has previously published two articles for *Fostering Families Today,* a magazine for foster families, and self-published a book entitled *Children in the Wind,* available through Amazon.com. She also plays drums on the worship team at her church.

Kathleen Tailer

Under the Marshal's
PROTECTION

Steeple
Hill®

Published by Steeple Hill Books™

STEEPLE HILL BOOKS

Steeple
Hill®

Recycling programs
for this product may
not exist in your area.

ISBN-13: 978-0-373-44415-1

UNDER THE MARSHAL'S PROTECTION

Copyright © 2010 by Kathleen Tailer

www.SteepleHill.com

Printed in U.S.A.

Be anxious for nothing, but in everything
by prayer and supplication, with thanksgiving,
let your requests be made known to God;
and the peace of God, which surpasses
all understanding, will guard your hearts
and minds through Christ Jesus.

—*Philippians* 4:6–7

For my husband, Jim, and all of my wonderful children: Bethany, Keandra, Jessica, Nathan, Joshua, Anna, Megan and James. You are all a tremendous blessing to me.

Also for my parents, Ken and Jane Ingham, who always supported me in every endeavor and encouraged me to reach for the stars.

ONE

Dominic knocked on the white screen door and took a step back. His eyes swept back and forth between the wide front porch of the aging country home and the spacious yard that surrounded it. An enormous live oak tree dominated the yard, and a wooden swing suspended from the lowest branch swung softly in the breeze. It was summertime in Tallahassee, Florida, and the grass was deep green and fragrant due to all of the recent afternoon rains. Dragonflies darted around the bushes, and a group of yellow butterflies congregated on the ground near the driveway. The setting was picturesque and almost looked like a Norman Rockwell painting.

It would have been a great place to sit and relax, if he wasn't on such an important mission.

Dominic turned and knocked again, bending slightly to see if he could catch a glimpse of anyone at home through the large open window. He didn't hear anything except his own feet making the porch floorboards creak and the soft squeak of the screen door as it moved slightly on its old rusted hinges.

He saw the barrel of the rifle out of the corner of

his eye just a split second before he heard the woman's threatening voice coming from the side of the wrap-around porch.

"Freeze, buddy."

He turned and raised his hands slowly. A woman dressed in faded jeans, an old burgundy T-shirt and a Florida State baseball cap approached him pointing a rifle straight at his heart. Her eyes were an electrifying blue that seemed to drill right through him. They were angry yet fearful at the same time, and her gaze swept over him very carefully, taking stock of him from head to toe. Her blond hair was pulled back and lay in a long braid down her back, and her lips were set in a thin line of determination. When she spoke, her voice was low and threatening. "You want to explain what you're doing on my front porch?"

Dominic kept his hands up, hoping his passive stance would put the lady at ease. "U.S. Deputy Marshal, ma'am. I just want to ask you a few questions."

The woman's eyes narrowed. "Prove it."

"Okay. I have my badge and ID in my back pocket. Can I reach for it without you shooting me?"

She eyed him warily but finally nodded, keeping the rifle trained on his chest. Dominic could tell she had noticed the 9 mm pistol strapped to his hip and was keeping a close eye on his hands. He slowly reached his right hand behind him and pulled out his ID wallet. He flipped it open and held it up to her.

"Drop it and step back."

Dominic obeyed, considering whether or not it was worth it to try to make a grab for the rifle when she picked up the wallet. Although he was sure he could overpower her and wrench the rifle out of her hands, from the way her eyes were filled with hard, gritty determination, he wasn't entirely certain he could do it without hurting her. He made his decision and took a step back, keeping his hands held high. At this point, it wasn't worth the risk. After all, she wasn't the fugitive he was searching for. She was just the missing man's sister.

He let her get the wallet without incident and watched as she examined his credentials. She looked back and forth between the photo on the ID and his face, her suspicious blue eyes carefully studying his features.

"I think you can get a badge like this on eBay for about five bucks."

Dominic shook his head and smiled, hoping to pacify her. "No, ma'am, you can't. It's a real badge, and I'm a real U.S. Deputy Marshal. Look, lady, if I wanted to hurt you, I would have done it already. I'm just here to ask some questions. That's it."

The rifle never wavered in her hands. "Just take your fake ID and get off my property. I don't want to answer any of your questions no matter who you are."

"Actually, you don't have a choice. Please put the rifle down, ma'am. You're threatening a law enforcement officer with a deadly weapon. That's a felony, you know."

He watched her eyes carefully and could see her actually considering his words and weighing out the truth of them. There was wariness in those blue depths, as well as a strength of purpose that he actually found himself admiring.

A moment passed, then another. Finally his words seemed to sink in, and she made her decision and took a step back. "I don't want any trouble. I just want you to leave. Like I said before, you need to just take your questions and get out of here." She motioned with the barrel. "Get off my porch. Now."

The balance of power seemed to shift ever so slightly with her small retreat. Dominic took advantage of it and took a step forward, then another. He was a large man, nearly a foot taller than the woman's five foot six inches, and he used his height to tower over her with an intimidating stance. He was focused on one thing and one thing only at the moment, and that was getting that rifle away from her before someone got shot.

"You can answer my questions here or you can answer them downtown. Either way, you're going to put that rifle down." He took another step. "You must be Jessica Blake. You're a schoolteacher, right? Well, Ms. Blake, like I said, you're assaulting a federal officer with a deadly weapon. All I want to do is ask you a few questions. Put the gun down." He paused, his hands still up in a sign of surrender. "Please, Ms. Blake. I'm not going to hurt you. I promise."

He watched her carefully, but her aim still didn't waver, despite his plea. What had her so spooked? The whole scenario didn't make sense. He could tell she was scared of him, but he couldn't figure out why. If she didn't think he was a legitimate marshal, who did she think he worked for?

"Ms. Blake, please give me a chance. I only need a few minutes of your time, and then I'll be out of here."

Jessica gritted her teeth and finally raised the barrel so it was no longer pointing at his chest. Her anger was evident in her stance, as was her fear. "You'd better not be lying."

Dominic swiftly eliminated the remaining space between them with two large steps and pulled the rifle from her hands, then flipped on the safety and ejected the cartridges. It was a Winchester .38 with plenty of kill-power, and he wasn't about to take any chances. When he was sure the gun was empty and safe, he handed it back to her but pocketed the bullets.

"Is that how you greet all of your visitors?" he couldn't help asking.

Jessica bit her bottom lip, suddenly appearing vulnerable for the first time in their encounter. She leaned the rifle against the wall and took a step back, then looked nervously around her as if seeking a route off the porch and into the trees if she needed one. She definitely didn't trust him, that was for sure, and Dominic wanted to know why. This was not the normal reaction he received when he was just out asking questions.

He took a deep breath, then slowly put his hands on his hips, trying to make his movements as nonthreatening as possible as he considered Jessica Blake. The woman before him was an enigma. He'd read all the information they had on her before coming. He knew her middle name, her date of birth, her social security number and all about the speeding tickets she'd gotten when she was sixteen. But nothing in her file mentioned just how striking her eyes were. He'd never seen anyone with eyes like that, and he felt a surge of attraction, even though she had a smudge of dirt on her cheek and was wearing faded and shapeless work clothes. Still, he couldn't help but notice the fine sheen of perspiration that covered her skin, in spite of the cool breeze.

Dominic studied her carefully from a law enforcement officer's perspective, trying to figure her out. She kept moving her hands in a nervous gesture, and her eyes were darting around as if she was expecting someone or something to jump out on the porch with them. There was clearly something going on here that was way out of the ordinary. He'd had guns pointed at him before, but certainly not by country schoolteachers with long blond hair and pretty blue eyes. The way she held herself and her expressions made it look as if she were hiding something, but Dominic had absolutely no idea what it could be. He had come expecting to ask a few questions and leave, but now he was intrigued, and couldn't leave until the puzzle of Jessica Blake was investigated and solved.

"Okay," she said roughly, breaking his train of thought. "You've got my bullets now. Ask your questions and be on your way, Mr. U.S. Deputy Marshal."

Dominic motioned toward the door, enjoying the way the words "U.S. Deputy Marshal" rolled off her tongue. She had the local Southern drawl, and without her threatening tone, her voice was now sweet and melodious, despite the slight tremor it still contained. He took a step toward her front door. "Could we sit down for a minute?"

Jessica shook her head and quickly blocked the doorway, nearly tripping as she hurried to keep him away from the door. What was inside that she didn't want him to see? Dominic raised an eyebrow.

"What's going on, Ms. Blake?"

Jessica shrugged, trying to appear carefree but failing miserably in the attempt. She was evidently not very good at subterfuge. "You said you only needed a few minutes. Just ask your questions out here."

Dominic sniffed. "Is that gas I smell? I think you might have a leak. That can be really dangerous, you know. I'd better take a look before the house explodes."

"Wait…" She grabbed his arm and pulled, but she was no match for his strength, and he moved effortlessly by her. He stopped just inside the door and froze, taking in the scene.

The place had been ransacked. The couch had been ripped to shreds, and foam stuffing was strewn throughout the living room. Glass dishes and knickknacks were smashed in little pieces all over, and books and a myriad of other items littered the floor.

He turned to Jessica, his eyes filled with concern. "Is there anybody else in the house?"

She shook her head. "Not anymore. I live alone, and whoever did this is long gone."

Dominic stepped over a broken radio and headed toward the kitchen. It too had been destroyed. The table and chairs were broken, and damaged appliances and

kitchen utensils had been dumped on the light blue lino-
leum floor. The cabinet doors were open, and canned
goods and staples had all been swept from their shelves.
He left the kitchen and slowly checked the rest of the
house. Each room had a similar level of destruction. It
looked as if a tornado had blown through and left nothing but devastation in its wake.

He blew out a breath and shook his head. No wonder
she was scared. Someone had definitely sent her a message, and he had the uneasy feeling that he knew exactly
who that someone had been. This case was getting more
complicated by the minute.

Jessica had followed him into the kitchen but didn't
follow him through the rest of the house. She went back
on the porch and waited patiently for him to come back
outside. She couldn't look at the inside of the house
anymore without crying anyway. Everything she owned,
with few exceptions, was now in pieces and totally
destroyed. What made it even worse was that there was
a law enforcement officer in there right now surveying
the damage, and she couldn't explain the mess without
putting her brother's life in danger.

She sank down on the steps, frightened and unsure.
It was all she could do not to grab her keys and drive
away as fast as her truck could carry her. But. There
was always a but. In this case, running wouldn't solve
anything. She knew that. She closed her eyes and leaned
against the front porch rail, rallying her strength for
the battle ahead and trying to figure a way out of her
predicament.

A few minutes later she heard the screen door open and close and the creaks of the porch as he crossed to sit down beside her. Several moments passed before he spoke. "That's quite a scene in there."

Jessica nodded without looking at him. It was hard to meet his eyes now that he'd seen the damage and would undoubtedly want an explanation. "That's why I didn't want you to go in there."

"Yeah, I guessed that." He paused. "Do you know who did it?"

"No."

"Do you know why they did it?"

Jessica took a deep breath. She didn't have any proof, but she had her suspicions. She didn't want to lie to the man, but until she knew more, she couldn't tell him the truth either. She chose to evade the issue. "Don't worry about it. It's my problem, okay?"

"No, it's not okay. Would you like for me to call in the crime tech guys and have them search for fingerprints? They might not find anything, but I'll make the call if you want me to."

For the first time, she met his eyes, deep gray and so gentle and concerned that she almost cried. But she couldn't trust him. She couldn't trust anyone when there was so much at stake. "No. I'm not filing a report or pressing charges. I'll deal with it myself. Like I said, it's my problem."

"Is that why you pointed your gun at me?"

She looked away again, embarrassed. She was a schoolteacher, after all. She didn't usually go around threatening people with a high-powered rifle, especially law enforcement officers. Deputy Dominic Sullivan was no small man either, and had broad shoulders and a muscular build that testified to his strength. His closely-cropped blond hair and chiseled features gave him a tough, military appearance, and the more she thought about it, the more she realized how foolhardy her actions had actually been. This man was a formidable foe. "Yes. I'm sorry about that." She could tell he wouldn't leave without a better explanation, but she also knew she'd have to keep it vague. "I was working out in the barn earlier when somebody hit me over the head and knocked me out. When I woke up, I came up to the house and found it like it is now. Then I heard you out on the porch, and I didn't know what to think."

Dominic gave her a friendly smile. "I'm sorry. I didn't mean to scare you." He paused, as if considering his options, then pushed forward. "I came here today because I'm looking for your brother Michael Blake. I need you to help me find him."

Jessica looked up quickly, her eyes filled with suspicion. "Why?"

Dominic drew his lips into a thin line. "Well, that's actually rather difficult to explain."

Jessica crossed her arms, undaunted. Why was a U.S. Marshal looking for her brother? She had to find out and make some sense out of everything that was happening to her today. "Why don't you try and simplify it for me?"

Dominic paused a moment, then nodded. "Okay. I can give you the basics. Michael Blake has been working at a company called Coastal up in Atlanta."

"Coastal? I've never heard of them before. What kind of company is that?"

"Pharmaceuticals. Sales and distribution, mostly."

"And?" she pressed.

"And he's gotten into some trouble with his employer, and I need to ask him some questions."

"Some questions about what?"

Dominic grimaced. "That's between me and your brother."

Jessica shook her head. "That's not good enough. I need to know what's going on."

Dominic raised an eyebrow. "What's going on, Ms. Blake, is that I have a warrant for your brother's arrest."

Jessica glared at him, then quickly stood and headed back in the house. She would have slipped back inside but Dominic was right at her heels and wouldn't let her avoid the situation by running away. He grabbed her arm gently and held her from escaping his questions.

"Ms. Blake. Please help me. Your brother's life may depend upon it."

She scowled at his hold, then raised her angry eyes to meet his. "You need to get off my property, Mr. U.S. Marshal. I have nothing more to say to you."

TWO

"Look. My name is Deputy Sullivan. Deputy Dominic Sullivan. I'm not the enemy. My job is to find Michael Blake and bring him in before he gets hurt. He's in a lot of trouble right now." He let go of her arm but remained blocking the doorway. "If you care about your brother, you'll help me."

"Goodbye, Mr. Sullivan. Thanks so much for stopping by." Her voice dripped with sarcasm, and her glare burned straight through him. Maybe from her point of view, he was the enemy after all.

"Wait," Dominic stated quietly, holding up his hands again in a motion of surrender. He couldn't just let her walk away. And he certainly wasn't going to leave her alone in that disaster area of a house. He changed tactics. "Are you sure you're not going to report this mess?"

Jessica nodded. "I'm sure." Apparently the last thing she wanted was even more policemen on her property.

"I'll help you clean up then." Before Jessica could even protest, Dominic passed into her house again and the screen door banged shut behind him, not quite masking the sound of Jessica's exasperated sigh behind him.

By the time she came back in, he had already righted the couch frame. With the cushions shredded, there wasn't much he could do for it beyond that, so he started putting books back on the shelves. "Any particular place you want these books?"

"What do I have to do to get you to leave?" she asked icily.

"I'm not going anywhere," he answered with another innocuous smile. He held out a stack of books. "So, where do you want these?"

Jessica shook her head wearily. Apparently she'd finally gotten the message that he wasn't going to go away. This was about more than finding Michael, however. There was no way he was going to leave Jessica Blake alone and terrified in her own home, especially without verifying who had done this to her house, and why.

"You don't give up easily, do you?"

Dominic grinned, hoping to thaw her resistance a little. Many people had told him he had a wonderful smile. He hoped that by using it now, he could break the ice with the woman before him.

He shook his head. "Now you're getting it."

The smile must have worked because she gave in with a sigh. "Just stack them back on that shelf, if you don't mind. I'll go get some trash bags and a broom."

Dominic smiled again, pleased at her surrender, and looked at some of the titles as he placed the books back on the built-in shelf. She seemed to own a large collection of mysteries, as well as an art history book or two and several books on drawing and painting. It appeared that Ms. Blake was an aspiring artist. He was pleasantly surprised by the revelation and actually a bit curious about her talent. He had a deep appreciation for art, even though he was convinced he had absolutely no talent of his own in that department.

Jessica returned with a medium-sized cardboard box and a large box of trash bags, then pulled out one of the bags and opened it with a snap. She handed the bag to Dominic. "Are you sure cleaning up my house is in your job description?"

He shrugged. "It is today."

If she couldn't get rid of him, she'd just have to ignore him. Turning her back on the marshal, Jessica started picking up the larger pieces of glass and other debris off the floor and tossing them into the cardboard box.

She hadn't owned anything of great monetary value, but she had attached great sentimental value to quite a bit in her home, and it was difficult to see it all destroyed. Nothing had been spared, including the decorative flowerpots that her fifth grade class had given her last year and the shiny blue ceramic bookends that had belonged to her parents. They were now in shards on the floor. The ruined couch cushions and pieces of stuffing started filling the bags, and tears came to her eyes when she tossed the broken frames that had been hanging on her walls into the box of trash. She quickly blinked the droplets away, determined not to cry in front of the law enforcement officer. There would be time to lament later. For now, she needed to concentrate on appeasing this marshal and getting him out of her house. She paused a moment and once again gingerly touched the bump on her head, then winced. The injury seemed to be throbbing more and more with each passing minute.

Dominic noticed. "Whoa there. Let's check that out." He reached for her arm and led her to sit in one of the few chairs in the home that hadn't been destroyed and gingerly removed her cap. "There's only a small cut, but that swollen knot on your scalp must be pretty painful. Stay right here and rest for a minute." He looked around the room, thinking. "I might have some aspirin in my car."

"There's probably a bottle in the bathroom medicine cabinet, if they didn't ruin that, too."

"Sounds good. I'll check it out." He left her and returned a few moments later with two aspirin and a glass of water. "Here. Take this." In his other hand he carried a plastic quart-sized bag filled with ice, covered with a damp washcloth. He watched her swallow the medicine, then gingerly placed the ice pack on her wound.

Jessica's eyes defiantly met his. "I'm still not going to answer your questions."

Dominic shrugged. "That's not my primary objective right now."

"What is your primary objective?"

"Helping you."

"Even if I refuse to help you?"

Dominic nodded. "Yes. Even if you refuse to help me."

Jessica let that sink in. When did anyone ever do something for nothing? She wanted to believe him, even though she was rather skeptical. She looked closely at the U.S. Marshal. There was concern in his eyes, but there was no way she could trust the law enforcement officer before her. She leaned back and closed her own eyes for a moment, the ice soothing the throbbing pain.

She had to handle this problem on her own. That was the bottom line. There was no one else to lean on, and this U.S. Marshal was certainly no knight in shining armor come to rescue her from her problems. Somehow, she would figure all this out and find a way to fix it. She had to. She had no other choice.

The phone suddenly rang, and she started in surprise. It rang again and she jumped up, frantically looking for the cordless receiver. She had been carrying the phone around with her for days ever since Michael's last call, but the events of the morning had thrown her out of her routine and she had to search to find where she had left the handset. She was so preoccupied that she didn't even notice Dominic stand up and follow closely behind her.

"Hello?"

The voice on the other end was low and threatening, and even though she didn't recognize it, it nonetheless sent a cold chill down her spine. "Jessica Blake?"

"Yes, this is Jessica."

"How do you like your house?"

She took a deep breath and her hands started shaking. "What do you want?"

"We want what your brother took from us. We want our computer disk back."

"What disk? I don't have your disk," she said forcefully, her voice tight. "I don't have a clue what you're talking about."

"It's very simple. We want what your brother took from us."

"I don't know where my brother is, or anything about what he took from you."

"Find it," the sinister voice ordered. "Find your brother, and find the disk. You have three days. If you don't return the disk, you'll be dead, along with your brother." There was a click, and Jessica knew she was alone on the line. Her ears started ringing and she felt incredibly light-headed. Her knees began to tremble and if Dominic hadn't caught her, she would have crumpled to the ground.

He carried her back over to the chair and set her down gently. Her whole body felt cold despite the June heat, and he rubbed her hands in a soothing gesture. "So? Who was that on the phone that scared you so badly?"

Jessica met Dominic's gaze, her own eyes rounded in fear and her breath coming in gasps. She shook her head, not knowing what she should do or say.

"Easy," Dominic soothed. "Take a deep breath." He demonstrated by exaggerating his breathing. She finally followed his lead and matched her breathing to his own.

"That's right. Take another deep breath. You'll be okay in a minute or two. Deep breaths. That's it."

Jessica concentrated on calming down, but the task seemed impossible. She was gripping Dominic's hands without even realizing it, and a numbing fear seemed to paralyze her. They were going to kill both Michael and her in three days if they didn't get what they wanted. She didn't doubt the caller's words for one minute. There had been a coldness in his voice that gave truth to his words.

She finally looked down and noticed their entwined hands and weakly tried to push his away. She didn't know this man, and in many ways, he seemed to be a threat to her as well. "You have to go now, Marshal. I need to be alone. I need time to think."

"No way," Dominic stated forcefully, clasping her hands and stilling their frantic motion. "You need to tell me what just happened on that phone call."

"I can't," she said softly, her voice shaking. "I can't tell you anything. Don't you see? They'll kill him, and they'll kill me, too."

"They'll probably try to do that now anyway." He squeezed her hands gently, but his stormy gray eyes were like steel. "You've just become a liability. These people don't leave a trail, Ms. Blake. They'll use you and dispose of you once you no longer serve their purpose. There's a bigger picture here that you don't understand. I can help you. The FBI and the Marshals have been going after these guys for a long time now. We know a lot about them and how they operate, but we can't get them to stop without your help." Their eyes locked and

Jessica felt as if the deputy could see straight into her soul. "Trust me," he pleaded quietly. "Let me help you, Ms. Blake. Please."

Jessica tightened her own grip on his hands and gritted her teeth. One thing she was sure of, she couldn't fight this threat on her own. It was too big, and she was going to need help. Men that killed on a whim were way out of her league.

She heard a small voice in her heart. *Come back to Me. Let Me help you.* She sighed inwardly and resisted the voice. She wasn't ready to let God back in her life. Not yet. The best she could do was grab hold of the hope that the marshal was offering.

"Promise me you'll help me save Michael," she whispered.

Dominic nodded. "I will do everything in my power to keep him alive."

Jessica shut her eyes, trying to gather the courage to trust the man before her. "I don't even know you," she said, more to herself than to the deputy who was kneeling by the chair.

"I'm sorry there isn't time for me to build your trust. I promise you, though, that I will do everything I can to keep Michael alive, and I'm a man of my word." He shifted, still not letting go of her hands. "Tell me about the phone call. Did you recognize the voice?"

Jessica shook her head, plunging ahead before she had time to really think and reconsider her actions. All the doubt and misgivings seemed to suddenly disappear as she opened her eyes and looked forcefully at the marshal. She was scared, and at the moment, Dominic seemed like her only option. She didn't really have a choice; not if she wanted to stay alive. "No. It was a deep male voice, that's about all I can tell you. He took credit for the damage to my house. Then he said that he wanted me to find some sort of computer disk. He said I had three days, and if I didn't give the disk back, then he would kill me and Michael, too." She swallowed convulsively. "I believe him. He'll come after us if I can't give him what he wants."

Dominic nodded. "Did he say anything else?"

"No, he just wants that disk." She locked eyes with Dominic. "What's on that disk?"

"Everything we need to convict the major players in a counterfeiting scheme, we hope." He gently squeezed her hands. "Ms. Blake, please tell me the truth. Do you know where Michael is?" He met her eyes with his own, probing.

Jessica bit her bottom lip. She needed this man's help. Michael needed his help. She had to trust someone. She took a deep breath and pressed forward, knowing full well that there was no going back once she had stepped over the line. "Michael called me a few days ago and told me that he was in serious trouble. He didn't go into details, but he asked me for help. We got cut off before we could finish our conversation. He sounded desperate, and I've been really worried about him ever since." She paused and looked away, then a moment later brought her eyes back to meet Dominic's once again. "I don't know where he is, but I have a cell phone number for him. I got the impression from some of the things he said that he's in the Tallahassee area, but I'm not sure. In the past, if I needed to contact him, I left him a message on his cell and he would always call me back, usually within an hour or so. Since I got that last call from him though, I've left a message every day, but he still hasn't called me back. I don't know what to think."

Dominic stood. "Does he normally call you back at your home number or on a cell?"

"Could be either, but I keep the cell charged and with me at all times, just in case."

"Good. Pack a bag. You're coming with me, and bring that cell phone and a charger with you."

Jessica stood, confused. "Where are we going?"

"To a safe house. I'm not taking any chances with you. Once you're protected, we'll have you call Michael with a frantic message of your own. When he calls, we'll use our equipment to trace his call and discover his location."

"You're not going to hurt him, are you?"

Dominic grimaced. "I don't want to hurt him, Ms. Blake, and neither do the people I work with, but he will be arrested. Michael is a fugitive, and it's my job to bring him in. Does he carry a gun?"

"He was carrying a pistol like yours the last time I saw him, but that was a long time ago. He's always liked hunting and is pretty good with a rifle." She came up to Dominic, stopping only inches away, and gave him a beseeching look. "I want to be with you when you arrest him. I want to make sure he's okay."

Dominic immediately shook his head. "That's not how it's done, Ms. Blake. You could get hurt or caught in the middle."

Jessica's eyes narrowed. "Then I'm not calling him," she said defiantly. "You need to meet my terms, Deputy. I have to be there. That's all there is to it."

"You're pushing too hard, Ms. Blake. I can let you talk to him after we have him in custody. That's the best I can do."

Jessica clenched her fists. "He's my brother," she said icily, her voice filled with determination. "If you can't meet my terms, then I'll go it alone."

"You don't know what you're saying," Dominic said roughly. "You have no idea how unscrupulous your enemy really is. You don't stand a chance without my help, and if you think about it, really think about it, you'll know that I'm right. If you try going it alone, you'll be dead in three days. That's a guarantee." He lowered his voice, his eyes intense. "You're really not in a position to be demanding anything, Ms. Blake. But I work with a good group of deputies. We always do our best to make our arrests in the safest way possible, for the suspect and for the deputies. I told you I'm a man of my word, and I meant it. I give you my word that we'll be as easy on him as we can. Our goal is to have him testify against Coastal. That company has been distributing counterfeit medicine on a huge scale, and from what we know so far, Michael was right in the thick of it. We want him on our side."

Jessica's eyes rounded. "What if he won't agree to go on your side?"

"Then he'll end up in prison, but at least he won't disappear without a trace or be murdered in the street. You'll know he's alive."

Jessica knew Dominic was right, but that didn't make it any easier to accept what he was saying. Oh, what she would give to start this day over! She looked into his stormy gray eyes and saw strength and professionalism, and she knew down deep that her choices were few. She sighed.

"All right, Marshal. I'll pack a bag." She grimaced, the full impact of his words weighing heavy on her mind. "How long should I plan on being away from my house?"

"Figure four or five days or so for now. If we need to, we'll find a washing machine somewhere." Dominic stepped back, looking relieved that she had agreed to work with him. He stood over her shoulder, watching her pack a duffle bag as if he expected her to change her mind at any moment and run. Well, if that was what he expected, he was in for a surprise. If the marshal was going to bring her brother in, then she wasn't going to let anything stop her from being by his side when it happened. Michael was *going* to live through this. She'd make sure of it.

And she'd work with whoever she had to in order to make it happen.

THREE

"So where is this safe house of yours?" Jessica asked quietly. Dominic was relieved to hear her speak. They had been driving for almost twenty minutes, but she hadn't said a word since they left her house. Her hands had been constantly in motion, however, and he'd seen her move a small, silver ring from finger to finger at least a dozen times.

"We're almost there," he assured her. "And in case you're wondering, you're doing the right thing."

She glanced out the window again, then turned and looked thoughtfully at the deputy. "I hope you're right." She bit her bottom lip. "What do you know about Michael? Tell me more about what he's gotten himself into."

Dominic straightened. "The charges against him are interstate counterfeiting medicine and conspiracy."

Jessica sighed heavily. "And you said all this happened in Atlanta?"

"That's right." Jessica winced and touched the sore on her head again. "But you said you were a U.S. Marshal. Why is a marshal interested in Michael? I thought you guys took care of the witness protection program and courthouse security, that kind of thing."

Dominic nodded. "We do those things, but we also collaborate with the FBI and other governmental agencies on certain cases and track down interstate fugitives. Michael was able to arrange a bond, but then he disappeared. We want him back."

"Well, what does counterfeiting medicine actually mean? I've never heard of that type of crime."

"It can mean a lot of different things. In this case, Michael has been working for a pharmaceutical company named Coastal Pharmaceuticals for about the last two years. Coastal owns several pharmacies in and around Atlanta, but they are also one of the major distributors in the business, and they supply medicines throughout the eastern seaboard. Apparently someone at Coastal has been diluting medicines, repackaging them and then selling the new bottles for profit."

"And the FBI thinks Michael is responsible?"

"If he isn't, then he knows who is," Dominic answered, his tone matter-of-fact. The district attorney had indicted four men in the Coastal case. Their first arrest had been Don Levine, a former Coastal employee, and when squeezed, Levine had pointed to Michael, Ross Kelley, who was Coastal's CEO, and Jeff Martin, Kelley's right-hand man, as the three other conspirators. A few days after the indictments had been handed down, Levine had been viciously murdered. Although the marshals didn't suspect Michael for the murder, they did believe that he had been a major player in the counterfeiting, just as Levine had suggested. The district attorney had leaned heavily on Levine's testimony for the indictments, and without him, the AG wasn't sure he could convict the other players. When Michael had been arrested, he had refused to talk to the feds, but when he had disappeared after he had bonded out of jail, rumor had it that he had disappeared with a computer disk filled with scans of paperwork that laid out the whole operation. That same disk and Michael's testimony could very well be the proof the FBI needed to reestablish their case and break up the counterfeiting ring once and for all.

Jessica shifted, frowning. "But Michael could be innocent, right?"

Dominic gave her a small smile at her hopeful tone. He could well understand why Michael's sister would want to defend him. She loved her brother. It was as simple as that. "We'll know for sure once we talk to him, but I wouldn't get my hopes up."

Jessica took a deep breath and wrung her hands. "Did anybody get hurt because of the bad medicine?" She stilled, waiting for his answer, looking incredibly afraid of what she would hear next.

"There was a boy who was hospitalized because of the switch, but so far, we're not aware of any fatalities. We don't know how much of the counterfeited medicine was distributed though, which is another reason why we need to talk to your brother. We need to find all of the diluted medicine that made it into the market before it does kill someone."

Jessica sighed with relief, but seemed to still be reeling from the magnitude of what Michael had gotten himself into. She pulled the silver ring off of her right hand and slipped it on to her left. "I doubt my brother could pull something like this off all by himself."

"I happen to agree with you, and so does the FBI, but like I said, we need to talk to Michael to discover the facts and find out the full extent of his involvement. We think Michael knows a lot of valuable information that could help us with our investigation of Coastal. He could very well end up being our key witness at trial if he cooperates."

"I can't believe he would be involved in something like this," Jessica said quietly, then slumped in her seat as the full implication of the deputy's words hit her. She closed her eyes and sighed heavily, then her eyes popped back open as a new thought occurred to her. "So why are you looking for him instead of a bail bondsman?"

Dominic shrugged. "The bondsman is probably looking for him too, but we do our own manhunts. Like I said, Michael could easily turn out to be the key witness in the investigation."

She raised her eyebrow, obviously churning all of this new information over and over in her mind. "Coastal is a legitimate company, right?"

"It appears to be from the outside, but we need to talk to Michael to see just how far inside the conspiracy has spread. Right now, it seems like there are only a few major players that are actually involved with the counterfeiting and distribution." He paused. "I know hearing all of this must be hard to swallow, but there is a lot more to it that I'm not at liberty to discuss." Don Levine's murder weighed heavily on Dominic's mind. The marshals were convinced that Ross Kelley at Coastal was the mastermind behind the whole scheme, and that Kelley had ordered Levine's death to protect himself once the counterfeited drugs had been discovered. If Kelley was silencing everyone who could testify against him, then Michael was definitely next on the list.

Dominic was also concerned about the mystery surrounding Levine's murder. Levine had been under police protection, yet he had still been viciously killed. How had the murderer gotten past the security detail? The case was still being investigated, but no matter what the result, the bottom line was that they needed to find Michael fast, for his sake, and to save their case against Coastal.

Dominic let the silence ensue for a moment, then stopped at a red light and turned toward his passenger. "So when was the last time you saw Michael?"

Jessica looked up and narrowed her eyes, apparently acutely aware that he had finished answering her questions and was now ready with some of his own. "It's been about a year, I guess."

The light changed and Dominic turned his eyes back to the road. "That surprises me. I thought you two might be closer than that."

"We used to be," Jessica said softly. "Believe it or not, Michael started out as a really good kid."

"What happened?" He knew a lot of Blake's background from the file, but it couldn't hurt to get his sister's side of things. In fact, he might just learn something important about his quarry.

"What happened is that my parents both died in a terrible accident and I was left to raise Michael. I did my best to give him a Christian home with Christian values. But somewhere during his high school years, I must have messed it up. Michael got in with the wrong crowd and started changing. At first he was just staying out too late, but one thing led to another, and he barely managed to graduate. He became sullen and defiant, and the older he got, the less he included me in his life. Then a few days after his commencement, he packed up his car and moved away from Tallahassee. I've heard very little from him since."

"How many times have you seen him since he moved out?"

Jessica sighed. "Only twice. He would never tell me much about his life or what was going on with him. Now I guess I know why." She closed her eyes for a moment, then continued. "I wish I'd had some help, you know? Like an uncle or an aunt to go to for help when his life started to get off track."

"You don't have any extended family?" Dominic asked, even though he already knew the answer.

"No one." She bit her bottom lip again and looked away. "Look, Michael has had his share of problems, but even when he turned sullen and secretive, I still always knew he had a good and gentle heart buried down deep inside."

Dominic didn't answer her, so she pressed on. "He's not a bad man, Marshal. You probably hear that all the time, but it's true. I know it in here." She tapped her chest for emphasis. "He must have just gotten mixed up in something bad and not known how to get out of it. He would never hurt someone intentionally. It's just not in him."

Dominic still didn't answer, and when she spoke again, her voice took on a desperate plea. "I don't think Michael can survive in prison, even if he was involved with the counterfeiting. I've seen the news, and Hollywood is filled with horror stories of what goes on behind bars." She paused for breath. "How long would he have to stay in prison if he gets convicted?"

"That all depends on the extent of his involvement and what he can testify to in court," Dominic answered. "It also depends upon what information he has on that disk. It must be valuable or Coastal wouldn't be going this far to retrieve it." He glanced at his passenger and noticed the turmoil that was etched into her face. It was obvious that Michael was in way over his head, and all of a sudden, so was she. This went way beyond teaching history and social science to fifth graders. When she had gotten up this morning, it had probably just been a normal Wednesday. Now her whole life was in shambles and she was filled with fear for herself and her brother. He decided a diversion was in order, and he swung through a drive-thru at the first fast-food restaurant he came across.

"What would you like? Once we get to the safe house, it may be awhile before we can grab something else."

She shook her head. "I'm not that hungry. I'm not even sure I can eat anything right now."

Dominic nodded, understanding. Her stomach was probably tied up in knots with worry and stress. "Okay, how about just a chocolate milkshake? That will at least keep you from starving." He gave her a grin, hoping to reassure her. What woman didn't like chocolate?

She hesitated but finally nodded, and he ordered the food, then paid and passed her the shake. He watched her carefully as she took her first sip and had to admit that she was handling everything he had told her today with amazing strength. Despite her negative assessment of her parenting skills, by all accounts Jessica had done a great job of taking care of Michael after their parents had died. She was seven years older than her younger brother and had worked hard to meet his needs, keep a job and put herself through school to earn her degree. According to his research, she had been a fifth grade teacher at the local elementary school for a few years, and apparently she raised and trained horses on the side now and then to supplement her income. Everyone spoke highly of her, and even he found himself admiring her and her accomplishments. Her life could not have been easy. He bowed his head and said a short silent prayer, both for the food, and to ask God to help Jessica persevere, then drove away from the restaurant and continued on his way to the safe house.

They were a few miles down the road before Jessica spoke again.

"So you're a praying man?"

Dominic nodded. "Yes, I'm a Christian. How about you?"

Jessica shrugged. "My parents took me to church when I was a kid, and I used to be really strong with my faith. After Michael started having problems, though, I pretty much fell away from it all. I ended up giving up on God since God seemed to have given up on Michael."

He took a sip from his drink and looked at her thoughtfully. "How did your parents die?"

"Car accident. I was nineteen. Michael was twelve. It turned my world upside down."

"I bet it did. I'm so sorry," Dominic said gently, his voice caring. "I know what it's like to lose a parent. My father died a couple of years ago and I still miss him. I guess I always will." He took a bite of his sandwich, then another swallow of soda. "Don't you miss having God in your life?"

She considered his words for a moment, then shrugged. "I don't know. I guess I haven't really thought about it in long time. I still pray sometimes, but my heart isn't always in it."

Dominic nodded. "Everyone goes through dry spells. If you ever want to get reconnected, there are some great fellowships here in town."

She smiled nervously at his enthusiasm, yet a wave of longing swept over her that took her by surprise. It had been years since she had gone to church on a regular basis, and she couldn't remember the last time she had cracked open her Bible. She still held on to her beliefs in some small part of her heart, but she hadn't practiced her faith in years. It had been too hard in the aftermath of losing her parents and watching Michael drift further and further away from her. She'd made up her mind that she wouldn't need anyone—not even God. But now she was wondering if she'd made the wrong decision. Would some of this mess be easier to bear with faith to see her through?

"I'll keep that in mind," she said softly. She took another sip from her milkshake, surprised that she was even discussing this subject with a virtual stranger. Something about this marshal was approachable and accepting. She usually didn't feel comfortable talking about her faith with anyone, but for some reason, talking to this man about the subject didn't make her feel odd. "Let me guess. You're one of those 'the glass is half full' guys, right?"

Dominic grinned. "How could you tell?"

She liked his smile. It lit up his entire face and made her feel like everything was going to be okay, even if the opposite was true and everything seemed to be falling to pieces around her. She took another sip, a small peace invading her. "Michael has made some bad choices. Sometimes I get really upset about him and the life he's chosen, and I feel responsible. What did I do wrong, you know? I tried my best to raise him, but look at him today. He's a fugitive and, according to you, responsible for putting counterfeit drugs on the market that are hurting people." She brushed the hair out of her eyes and blinked back tears. "How could he really be involved with something like that? I just don't know how he could do such a thing."

"Your parents taught him right from wrong and gave him a strong foundation. You supported him along the way. At some point, Michael has to take responsibility for the choices he makes, as well as the consequences of his actions. You can't live his life for him."

"Deep down, I know you're right, but it doesn't make it any easier to accept. I want the people I care about to be successful and happy. I love him too much to see him throw everything away like this." A silent tear rolled down her cheek, but she wiped it away angrily and resolved not to cry in front of the stranger. The marshal seemed like a nice enough man, but he was clearly interested in finding Michael because of his job, not because he truly cared about him. It was up to her to look out for Michael's best interests. But how could she do that without talking to Michael first? She wished she could know more about what was really going on and hear his side of the story. She pulled out her cell phone and double-checked that it was on and the batteries were fully charged. She needed to talk to Michael. Then somehow, someway, they were going to make it through this. All she needed now was to figure out how.

FOUR

Jessica paced back and forth in the narrow hotel room, thinking that if she stayed in this small space much longer, she was going to go stir crazy. She'd been here for two days already, and the waiting was starting to get to her. A hotel room was a hotel room. There wasn't much to do except watch TV, and she found little pleasure in television, even if she did have fifty channels to choose from. She had made six desperate calls to Michael in the last twenty-four hours, but so far she still hadn't heard from him. The fact that he hadn't responded made her wonder if Michael was even still alive, especially knowing what she did about Coastal and the danger he was in. The fear twisted in her stomach and made it even harder for her to sit still in the small, confining room.

During her short time in protective custody with the marshals she had met two new deputies. Jake Riley was apparently the technology expert and had all the equipment set up to trace the call if and when Michael finally contacted her. He also seemed to be the leader of the group but let the others do their jobs with very little interference. Dominic and Chris Riggs had been taking turns keeping watch over Jessica and continuing their search for Michael via other means. They had tracked down an address where Michael had lived two months ago in a small suburb of Atlanta, and had local deputies talking to neighbors and trying to discover where he had moved to next. It was tedious work, and Jessica could tell from their discussions that their leads were fading fast. She was definitely their best chance at finding her brother.

A knock at the door sent Chris to the peephole, and a few seconds later Dominic entered carrying breakfast and a plain brown paper sack. He passed out warm sausage biscuits and coffee, then little packages of sugar and cream to those who wanted them.

"What, no donuts?" Jessica joked. She was surprised by how glad she was to see him. Although she had only known him a short time, she felt inexplicably safer with him nearby.

"Funny," Dominic smiled, then handed the paper sack to Jessica. "I know you're bored. I got these for you to help pass the time."

Jessica opened the sack and was surprised to see a selection of mystery novels by her favorite authors whose books had lined her shelves at home. She was truly touched by his thoughtfulness. There was even a book about drawing technique and a small sketch pad with pencils included in the bag. "I can't believe you noticed," she said with a smile. "Thank you so much."

"You're welcome, Ms. Blake." He grinned at her. "I've done this enough to know that it takes more than a TV to pass the time."

So he had noticed that, too. "Please call me Jessica." She grinned back at him and felt herself actually relaxing for the first time since she had come to the hotel.

Suddenly her cell phone rang, and she jumped, then grabbed it and looked at the caller ID. "I don't know the number."

Dominic gently touched her shoulder. "It's okay. Answer anyway." They had already established that several of Jessica's friends called her cell phone number on occasion. The call could be coming from any one of them.

Jessica nodded and pushed the answer button on her phone. "Hello?"

"Jess! Are you all right?"

Jessica sank down to the bed. The speaker was young and frantic, and it was unmistakably the voice of Michael Blake. She nodded to Dominic who had picked up a headset and was listening to the call. Across the room, Jake started to run the trace.

"I'm okay, but, Michael, somebody came to my house and tore it apart. Then they called and threatened me. They said you stole some sort of computer disk. Michael, did you do that?"

"Oh, Jess, I'm so sorry. I had no idea this would come back on you."

Jessica sighed. "Michael, answer my question. Do you have their disk? What's all this about?"

A beat passed, then another. "I can't explain right now. It's…it's complicated."

Jessica noted that Michael's voice had changed and a wave of dread swept over her. His tone was hesitant, and he was obviously avoiding the truth. It wasn't the time or place to argue about it, though. Somehow she needed to convince Michael to turn himself in. Then they could sort all of this out together once and for all. She looked over at Dominic who was motioning with his hands to keep the conversation going.

"Michael, I need to see you. Tell me where you are."

Again there was silence on the other end of the line. Finally, he spoke. "I can't, Jess."

"You don't have a choice," she answered vehemently. "They said they were going to *kill* you and me in two more days if you didn't give them the disk. I need to understand, Michael. I want to try to help you."

"Oh, Jess…"

"Tell me where you are. I'll come and get you and we'll figure this out together."

Dominic shook his head at this one, but Jessica pushed forward, ignoring him. "Michael, I don't want you to get killed, and I'm in no hurry to die, either. This is a huge problem you can't deal with by yourself. Let me help you. Please."

Silence met her plea for such a long time that she thought he might have hung up. Finally, he spoke. "Are you still at the house?"

"No, I didn't feel safe there, so I'm in Tallahassee with friends. They tore up my home pretty badly anyway. There's not much left."

"Meet me at the bagel shop in two hours. You know which one. Come alone, Jess. Don't bring your friends." The phone clicked, and Michael was gone.

* * *

Dominic was furious, but doing his best to hide it. He paced a few times, then strode over to Jake. "Did we get him?"

Jake shook his head. "He's in northern Tallahassee, but I didn't have enough time to narrow the field any closer than that."

Dominic paced some more. What was Jessica doing, arranging to meet Michael in person? The last thing he wanted was to include her in the arrest. Involving civilians in arrests was unpredictable at best, and downright dangerous at worst. He rubbed his neck with his hand and rounded on her. "What were you thinking? I told you that you weren't going to be a part of this and I meant it."

Jessica stood and put her hands on her hips. "And I told you I'm his sister, and I want to make sure that he doesn't get hurt."

"This isn't the way we do things, Ms. Blake."

"So we're back to 'Ms. Blake' again, are we?"

Dominic gritted his teeth. "You're not listening to me."

"No, you're not listening to me," she said forcefully, poking him in his chest with her finger. "He's my brother, and I'm the one who is being threatened. I'm involved already, and I'm going to stay that way. Especially when it comes to bringing my brother in. You don't even know what bagel shop to go to without my help. You need me."

Dominic took a step forward so that he was mere inches away from her. He towered over her in an intimidating stance. "Actually, you need me," he said in a deceptively soft tone. "I'm the one trying to keep you and Michael from getting killed, remember? A little cooperation here wouldn't be out of line."

She had to bend her neck back to meet his eyes, but she did it, her own eyes spitting blue fire. "Yes, I remember. And I'm the one betraying my own brother. Did you remember that?"

He acknowledged that she had a point, but he still didn't like it. Unfortunately, she had left him with little choice. Two hours was barely enough time to get a plan together for an arrest in such a public location. Finding an agent to be her double just wouldn't be possible in that time frame. He narrowed his eyes and when he spoke, his voice was deadly serious. "You will obey every command I give you out there, do you understand?"

She nodded, clearly knowing she had won, but wanting to leave his pride intact. "Yes, I understand. I'll do whatever you ask."

Dominic straightened, then grimaced. "Okay. To start with, tell me which bagel shop we're talking about. We need to plan this out."

They sat down across from Jake and Chris and started talking over their strategy. Chris was assigned the task of going immediately to the bagel shop so he could call them and give them the lay of the land, as well as establish himself as a customer. Jake called and coordinated their efforts with the local police department and made sure they had communication devices so they could all keep in contact. Dominic went over the plan with Jessica until he was sure she was prepared for every contingency. He was still uncomfortable with having her participate with the arrest, but couldn't convince her to stay at the hotel, even by promising her a chance to talk to Michael after he was taken into custody.

Dominic had no choice but to move forward with the plan, and hope that the sinking feeling in his stomach wasn't a sign that everything was about to go terribly wrong.

What seemed like only a short time later, a female marshal named Whitney Johnson, dressed in civilian clothing, dropped Jessica off in front of the bagel shop. The two women waved at each other as if they were old friends, then Jessica turned and glanced around the parking lot. The bagel shop was at the end of a busy strip mall that housed several different boutiques and two larger clothing stores. The lunch crowd was starting to come in, and several of the wrought iron tables on the sidewalk outside the store were already filled with customers enjoying their designer café and deli sandwiches. Jessica saw Chris eating alone at one of the tables. He appeared to be engrossed in a magazine and didn't acknowledge her, nor did she expect him to.

She opened the door and went inside, again noticing that the place was busier than she expected. The shop had about fifteen small tables that each seated either two or four customers, and at least half of the tables were filled with a wide assortment of people. One little girl, approximately four years old, was bouncing around a table next to her mother who was trying to spoon-feed some baby food to a fussy infant. Two older men were playing chess in the corner, and four lively women were having a vibrant conversation about local politics at another table. She studied the faces of the other customers but didn't see her brother yet. Hopefully he would get here soon, and this whole affair would be over. She dreaded Michael's arrest, but she had to agree it was definitely better than finding him dead in an alley somewhere.

Customers waited cafeteria-style for their turn in line so they could have their food made to order, and she joined the line, waiting for her turn. Racks of bagels lined the walls behind the counters, and twin refrigerated compartments, containing various beverages for sale as well as fruit and tubs of eight different flavors of cream cheese, met customers before they reached the cash register. Jessica studied the menu that plastered the wall above the bagel racks. Although her stomach was in knots, she wanted to order something so that she would blend in with the other customers. She finally chose a chocolate chip bagel with low-fat cream cheese and a cranberry juice, then paid the cashier and took her snack to a table near the back that faced the front door. She wanted to have a clear view of everyone who went in and out of the restaurant, and this table seemed to have the perfect vantage point.

The little bell over the door rang and caught her attention, and she noticed Dominic come in. He was dressed very casually in jeans and an old polo shirt with a faded Marlins baseball cap pulled low over his eyes. Even in that getup, he was incredibly handsome. She quickly looked away, but not before a whisper of attraction swept through her. She grimaced, unhappy with the direction her thoughts had taken her. Since when was she attracted to pushy law enforcement officers? She shrugged to herself and kept an eye on the door, bringing her thoughts back to the task at hand.

Each time the bell rang she waited expectantly, hoping that she would see her brother's face come through the door. She didn't have long to wait. After about ten minutes, a rangy blond man walked in wearing khaki shorts, a long-sleeved navy button-down shirt, a fishing hat and a pair of dark tortoiseshell sunglasses. He was thin, probably a little too thin by Jessica's estimation, and his face was haggard and covered in a scraggly beard and mustache, but there was no hiding his identity from his sister. He noticed her right away and went directly to her table. Jessica jumped to her feet and gave him a rambunctious hug.

"Michael! Thank God! I was so worried about you."

"Hey, Jess. Thanks for coming."

They sat down and in her exuberance, Jessica knocked over her drink. Michael jumped back, missing the spray of cranberry juice, just as the first bullet drilled into the wall behind him.

FIVE

The second bullet nicked Jessica in the arm as the two dove for the ground and pushed the table over to use it as a shield. Utter chaos reigned. People were screaming as another gunshot was heard by the front door, and the shooter went down hard. Jessica felt a heavy weight over her and realized Dominic had crawled over and was protecting her body with his own. Their eyes met—Jessica's filled with fear and Dominic's filled with worry.

Jessica looked toward where Michael had landed but saw no sign of her brother. The long-sleeved navy shirt he had been wearing was in a heap on the floor, as well as the sunglasses and hat. She looked around the bagel shop—at least, as much of it as she could see from this angle. Most of the patrons had taken refuge under their tables, but screaming continued and several people had run out of the restaurant through the back emergency exit, which had set off an obnoxiously loud shrieking alarm.

Dominic pulled back, visually checking her for other injuries. "Are you okay?"

She nodded, then winced as she moved her arm. Her

entire shoulder was throbbing. "Michael is gone." She looked down at her wound and for the first time seemed to notice that blood was seeping through her fingers. "Wow. That really hurts."

Dominic glanced around, his weapon drawn, but seemed to calm down as he realized that nobody else had fired since the man near the door had gone down. Jessica guessed that meant the downed man was a lone shooter. Dominic returned his weapon to his ankle holster and turned his attention back to Jessica. "Hopefully, someone grabbed Michael on his way out. I don't think he was injured." He examined her bleeding arm, then pulled out a handkerchief and applied pressure to the wound. "Hold this on it. You're going to need a few stitches, but the bullet just grazed you." He gave her a smile. "It looks a lot worse than it is, I promise. You're really going to have to stop trying to catch bullets with your arm." He brushed the hair out of her eyes. "Will you be okay for a minute or two while I check in with everybody?"

Jessica nodded while Dominic spoke into a small microphone that he had clipped on his shirt and listened intently to the small earpiece that connected him to the other marshals outside. He reported Michael's disappearance and Jessica's wound, then sat silently for a moment as he listened to the other reports coming in. He gave her a piercing look. "It's over. Michael escaped. Stay here and sit tight while we try to calm everybody down. Then we'll get you to a hospital so we can take care of that arm." He reached for her hand and squeezed it, then stood and started walking around the tables.

She watched as he went from person to person, identifying himself and reassuring them as he helped them get to their feet and settle down. She couldn't help but be impressed by the care and concern he showed as he gently led them to the front door and tried to block their vision as best he could of the dead shooter lying on the floor. Every few seconds he glanced back at Jessica to make sure she was still where he had left her.

Chris and Jake were also talking to customers and the restaurant staff, and Jessica saw that the initial officers from the Tallahassee Police Department had arrived on the scene and were also interviewing people outside. Suddenly the alarm was silenced, and she could hear sirens outside just barely above the din of voices and other noise in the restaurant.

She looked over at Michael's abandoned clothes and glasses. Upon closer inspection, she noticed what looked like a wad of hair and glue near the shirt. Apparently Michael had learned a thing or two about disguises, and the scraggly beard and mustache had been fake. After the first bullet had been fired, he must have changed his appearance and his clothing so he could slip out unnoticed during all of the confusion. She had to give him credit for thinking ahead and having an escape plan in the first place. Obviously, he knew his life was in danger and had prepared for that contingency. She, however, was not used to living in fear. Her hands started shaking as the full impact of what had just happened hit home and the adrenaline surge started to ebb.

Apparently someone had known Michael was going to be at the bagel shop today and wanted him dead right away. Did that mean Coastal had already found the disk, and his life was now worthless to them? Had the shooter been trying to kill her as well? She needed to talk to Michael and get some insight, but would he trust her again? Question after question came rushing to her mind. She tried to take a deep breath to calm herself, but she couldn't seem to stop shaking.

Everything she knew in her life had come crashing down within the last forty-eight hours. She had never bothered anyone and had always lived a quiet existence. How could someone suddenly be trying to kill her?

Jessica had been wrong. She couldn't handle this situation on her own, or even with the marshal's help. Dominic was doing his best to protect her, but he was only a man and could only do so much. She needed more than just someone to keep her safe anyway. If nothing else, the last few hours had shown her with absolute clarity that she needed God back in her life, and the pull on her heart was strong. This time, she wasn't going to resist.

Jessica closed her eyes and took a deep breath. Her prayer was short but heartfelt. *I know I was wrong to shut You out, Lord. I'm so sorry. Thank You for not giving up on me and for loving me, even though I've stayed away for so long. Please forgive me for my mistakes and come back into my life.* She slowly opened her eyes and felt a warm, peaceful feeling come over her. For the first time, she finally understood that God wasn't going to erase her problems, but that He would always be there to go through the problems with her. It was a very comforting thought.

Finally, Dominic returned to her side and strong arms lifted her to her feet. Instinctively she leaned into his strength, raising her head to give him a weak smile of thanks. He met her eyes and seemed to see that something had changed. "Are you okay?"

Jessica gave a small laugh. "Actually, I feel better than I've felt in years. God is good, did you know that? I just felt His presence for the first time in a very long time."

Dominic smiled and squeezed her hand. "That's really good to hear," he said, beaming at her.

"Now, it's time to get you to a doctor. Come on, let's get you out of here."

Dominic's admiration for Jessica went up another notch when her spine noticeably stiffened and she gained control of her shaky emotions. This was one tough lady. It was horrible that something so violent had happened to her, yet he couldn't help being pleased that it had brought her back to God. It was always amazing to him that what men meant for evil, God could use for good.

He led her out the back door of the restaurant so they wouldn't have to walk past the dead body and also to avoid the gathering crowd that was filling up the parking lot. Chris was just getting out of the car he had brought around for them when they arrived. He tossed the keys to Dominic, gave him a nod and headed back into the bagel shop. The other marshals would be there for a while as they processed the crime scene with the local police. Even the FBI had joined the party and had sent over their liaison, since they were also working on the

Coastal task force. But Jessica Blake was Dominic's responsibility, and right now that meant getting her out of there.

"Stay safe," Chris said over his shoulder.

"You too," Dominic answered. He opened the door for Jessica, got her situated and then circled the car. A few moments later he got behind the wheel and pulled away from the parking lot, leaving the aftermath behind them. He constantly surveyed the road and surrounding area as he drove, keeping his eyes open for threats as they headed to the hospital.

"So what happened back there?" Jessica asked quietly.

"Someone from Coastal must have found out about the meeting."

"How?"

Dominic shrugged, but nonchalance was the last thing he was actually feeling. In fact, the same question was eating at him. How had Coastal found out? For now, he wanted to reassure Jessica, but at some point, that question would have to be answered. "We may never know. My instincts tell me Michael wasn't careful enough when he was making his calls. We were tracking him, so it's a good bet that Coastal was on to him too. We haven't identified the shooter yet, but I'm guessing he's a hit man hired by Ross Kelley, the CEO of Coastal. One thing I can pretty much guarantee is that the shooter didn't know we would be there."

He paused and took a deep breath. He would sort out the rest of this after he got Jessica the medical attention she needed. "It's a good thing we were with you. If we hadn't been watching and taken the shooter down when we did, a lot more people could have gotten hurt." He met her eyes. "Including you."

Jessica's crystal blue eyes met his and a shiver of awareness swept through him. He was almost afraid to look away, needing the reminder of those vivid, vibrant eyes to prove to himself that she was alive and well, that the shooter hadn't seriously injured her. It had been a close call—too close. Upset at the thought, Dominic turned his attention back to the road just as the light changed.

"You're right, of course," Jessica replied. She continued to press the handkerchief against her wound. "But Michael is still out there by himself, and I might have just lost his trust. Do you think he'll call again?"

"We won't know what's going on in his head until we can get him in a dialogue. As soon as we get back to the safe house, we'll have you call him to set up another meeting and see if he responds." He glanced at Jessica again, noticing the fear etched in her features. "Don't worry. He's smarter than I thought and came to the meeting with an escape plan. He seems to have a few tricks up his sleeve, and hopefully that will buy him some time."

"How can they expect to get their disk back if they kill him?"

"I think right now they're more worried about him telling what he knows about their operation. They want that disk back so it can't be used as evidence against them, but at this point they probably figure the disk will never surface if they can take Michael out of the picture. They've already killed one witness. To them, what's one more?"

Jessica sighed. "I don't even know if Michael will testify. What makes them, or you, for that matter, so sure that he will?"

"They probably don't know one way or the other, but they might be thinking he's not worth the risk. I told you before that you can't underestimate these people. It might be the last thing you ever do."

A Tallahassee Police Department officer met them at the emergency room entrance and helped clear the way for Jessica's medical treatment. The bullet had ripped the skin on her arm near her shoulder, but it was just a flesh wound, and after giving her sixteen stitches and a prescription for antibiotics, she was ready to go. Dominic stopped at a drugstore, and they got her medicine and some aspirin, then headed back to a different hotel room in a different part of town. He hadn't seen any sign that they were being followed, but he wasn't taking any chances with Jessica's safety.

Once they got settled in a room, Dominic checked in with Chuck Holiday on a secure line to let him know their whereabouts. Chuck was the FBI agent assigned to the task force and was just finishing up at the crime scene. After they finished their short conversation, Dominic sat back in the desk chair and dialed Jake.

"Hey. We're at the Rhalston Hotel. Can we rendezvous in two hours?"

Jake paused. "Better make it three. Chris was the one who actually took out the shooter, so he's still wading through the paperwork. It will be a while longer before he's free. You know how those reports go on forever." He cleared his throat. "We ran a fingerprint check on the downed man. His name was Davis Sanders. Turns out he was a small-time drug dealer from Atlanta who was also a suspect in two other shootings. We're still trying to connect him to Kelley or Coastal, but I'm not surprised that the connection isn't immediately apparent. Kelley seems to be an expert at covering his tracks, and so far, he's made very few mistakes."

Dominic agreed. "This attack makes it crystal clear that we have to get Michael Blake into custody as soon as possible. Kelley is obviously willing to put innocent civilians at risk in order to have Michael silenced."

"You've got that right. You know, Levine's death was suspicious, but it looks even more suspect in light of what happened today at the bagel shop."

Dominic grimaced. "I told Ms. Blake that Coastal had tracked Michael through his phone, but if we look at that combined with the circumstances surrounding Levine's death, it seems highly unlikely." He raked his fingers through his hair, then stood and started pacing like a caged lion. "Jake, I hate to even suggest it, but do you think we have a leak somewhere who's funneling Coastal information?"

There was silence on the other end of the phone as both men considered the implications. The thought was disturbing to say the least. Law enforcement personnel were like one big family. It was inconceivable that one of them was selling information to the highest bidder. Still, they couldn't ignore the facts before them.

"I'm going to have to think on that for a while," Jake said slowly. "Let's keep the idea to ourselves until we can flush it out."

"Agreed," Dominic said pensively. "See you in three hours." He hung up with Jake but kept pacing as the thoughts spun around in his head. He made a mental list of those who knew of both Levine's whereabouts while he was in custody and the bagel shop incident. There were at least fifteen people among the different law enforcement agencies that could be responsible for selling Coastal information. The Coastal task force was large and had involved a series of agencies from the local and federal levels. Somehow he would have to narrow that number down. He was hoping that he was wrong—but he knew enough to prepare for the worst, all the same.

He looked over at Jessica, who had collapsed in a chair by the curtained window. She had her eyes closed and looked sweet and vulnerable. He'd only met her two days ago, but he couldn't remember ever being so impressed by a woman before. Sure, he knew lots of women, but none had ever had Jessica's spirit. He grinned, remembering how she had threatened him with her rifle on her front porch. Yes, Jessica had spunk, that was for sure. She was also one of the most attractive women he'd ever met. If things were different… He clenched his jaw. Jessica was a witness. No more, no less. The day he lost his objectivity was the day he needed to find someone else to protect her.

He thought about the leak and a wave of anger swept over him. Law enforcement officers were supposed to protect the people, not put them in greater danger. Now the risks to Jessica's life were doubled.

He clenched his fists and paced some more. What would he do if the threats to her escalated even further? Would he be able to keep her safe? He needed another backup plan, just in case, and his mind started sorting through the possibilities. One way or another, Jessica Blake was going to live through this ordeal; of that he was certain.

SIX

Ross Kelley unbuttoned his blazer and sank down into his plush leather office chair. He had worked hard to become the CEO of Coastal and was proud of the magnificent corner office that was a small but necessary perk of his position. He glanced up at his diploma that proclaimed he was a graduate of an Ivy League school, and at his pharmacy license, both of which had been richly framed and decorated the wall for all to see. He wasn't about to let all of his hard work and effort get taken away from him by some young, no-account punk kid from Florida.

Besides, Michael Blake made the perfect patsy to take the blame for the entire counterfeiting scheme. Kelley was well on his way to framing the younger man for the entire operation. If he played his cards right, Kelley could keep the millions he'd made from the counterfeiting tucked safely away in the Caymans while Blake met the same fate as Levine. Without Blake in the picture, the district attorney would be forced to dismiss the charges against Kelley. It was as simple as that. Kelley hadn't started out to kill anyone, but he would do whatever was necessary to protect what was his. In fact, ordering Levine's death had given him a rush of power flowing through his veins that had made him feel nearly indestructible. Now he held Michael Blake's life in the palm of his hand, and he liked it. With an economy of motion, he leaned back and caught the eye of his right-hand man, Jeff Martin. Martin came to the edge of Kelley's desk, bringing an espresso in a small china cup and setting it on the desk before him.

"Well?" Kelley questioned, reaching for the cup and taking a sip.

Martin shook his head. "It didn't happen."

Kelley choked on the coffee and slammed the cup down on the table. Murky brown liquid splashed across the papers on the desk and burned the tender skin on the back of his hand as the cup shattered into a thousand pieces. "Why not?"

"Incompetence."

"I hope the man you sent is no longer in our employ."

Martin smiled. "He's nobody's problem at this point. He was killed by an off-duty cop."

Kelley nodded. "Interesting."

"Should we hire someone to replace him?"

Kelley picked up a napkin from his desk and mopped the coffee he had spilled. He hadn't become CEO of one of the largest pharmaceutical companies in the nation by backing down at the first sign of trouble. He wasn't going to start now. The last thing he needed was Michael Blake talking to the authorities. He knew too much about their operation. It had been foolish to bring him into the counterfeiting scheme in the first place, but they had needed somebody to do the grunt work, and Levine had made the poor decision to bring Michael Blake on board. Levine would never make that or any other mistake again. Unfortunately, before Levine had died, he had spoken to the FBI, and both Kelley and Martin were still facing their indictments. He eyed Martin speculatively. Martin had worked with him for over ten years, and he was one of the few men in the world that Kelley actually trusted. Martin would never roll on him if times got tough. He had proven himself time and time again. He met Martin's eye.

"Definitely. I want this problem to disappear. Do you understand me?"

"What about the disk?"

"Find it if you can, but I want this hole plugged before the whole ship starts floundering." He stood and met Martin's eyes. "Have the feds found the trail we planted? I want more than just the charges dropped. I want a public apology from the district attorney himself."

"Everything is going according to plan. All of the phony invoices were planted, and our computer tech fixed the rest. Everything is pointing directly to Blake. Your attorney also confirmed that Levine's grand jury testimony can't be used against you at trial. Their entire case is quickly going up in smoke."

Ross Kelley smiled confidently. He wasn't a man who left anything to chance, and it seemed like he had all of his bases covered. He also never underestimated the value of getting his information from a variety of places.

"What about our contact on the inside?"

"Still in place, but asking for more money. I think he's getting a little greedy."

"Pay him. We still need him for now."

Martin shifted. "What do you want to do about the sister?"

Kelley leaned back in his chair, his expression thoughtful. What was one more life? He had to protect his financial future, not to mention keeping himself out of prison. "Eliminate her, too. Like I said, I want the hole plugged. No loose ends. Who knows what Blake might have told her?"

"You got it," Martin nodded. "Consider it done."

The cell phone vibrating in her hand woke Jessica up from a doze. She shifted uncomfortably in the chair, then looked over to Dominic, who was sitting at the desk in the hotel room. He motioned for her to answer the phone as he flipped a switch on his handset and adjusted his earpiece so he could listen in on the call. She opened the cell and pushed the receive button, even though it was another number that she didn't recognize.

"Hello?"

"Jess." Michael's voice was soft at first and barely audible.

Jessica jumped to her feet. "Michael? Is that you?"

Jessica noticed Dominic's instantly alert posture. If she could keep him on the phone long enough, they could get a fix on his location and still have a chance of taking him into custody.

"Yeah, it's me." His voice was stronger now. "What happened at the bagel shop?"

Jessica sighed. "I was going to ask you that question. Who was that guy with the gun?"

"A better question is who was the guy that killed him?"

Jessica glanced over at Dominic. She wasn't sure if the deputy wanted her to reveal their relationship, but she couldn't lie to her brother. Michael wasn't stupid either. He had to know something more was going on than what she had disclosed. Before she could think of an appropriate answer, Michael asked another question, concern filling his voice.

"Is your arm okay? I know he shot you."

"Yeah. I got a few stitches, but I'm doing fine."

"I'm sorry I left you like that, Jess. I got scared."

"It's okay, Michael." She took a deep breath. "Look, it's obvious that you're in real trouble. I still want to get together so we can talk all this out. Those guys who threatened me only gave me three days to give the disk back. Since they were trying to kill us, does that mean they've already got it?"

Michael took a moment to answer. "No," he said finally. "They don't have the disk. I think they've decided they just want to shut me up."

"Tell me about the disk, Michael. What's on it that is so all-fire important that they're willing to kill to get it back?"

"It's filled with business documents, Jess. Proof that the heads at Coastal counterfeited medicines and distributed them. You can make a lot of money if you dilute some of the really expensive stuff and sell it off as the real deal."

Jessica's heart started beating faster. "Michael, tell me the truth. Were you part of the counterfeiting, too?"

Michael paused. "I can't tell you what you want to hear, Jess. I needed the money."

Pain swept through her so swiftly she had to sit down. "Michael, we have to go to the police."

"I'm not ready to do that, Jess."

"You can testify in court and put the people who started this whole mess in prison. If you turn over that disk to the authorities, you can make some kind of deal."

Michael blew out a breath in exasperation. "Who are you working with, Jess?"

Jessica met Dominic's eye, her expression unsure. Could she tell him? Dominic paused a moment, then nodded. Her shoulders dropped in relief. Subterfuge had never been her strong suit. "U.S. Marshals. They're part of a multiagency task force that has been investigating Coastal for months. Michael, they want you to come in and testify against the drug company."

"I bet they do," Michael said quietly. "Look, I'm sorry you got dragged into this. I really am." He groaned. "Are they listening to this call right now?"

Again, Jessica looked at Dominic for a cue, and again he nodded. "Deputy Sullivan is listening. He's the one who took me to the hospital to get my arm stitched up."

Her response was initially met with silence, but finally Michael spoke. "Listen, Sullivan, I get what you want, but I also know what happened to Levine. You can't protect me, and if you let anything happen to my sister I'll come after you myself."

Dominic straightened but let the threat pass. "You're out of options, Michael. Coastal wants you dead. They made that obvious enough at the bagel shop. We can protect you."

"Like you protected Levine?"

"That's still being investigated."

"Yeah, I hear you. I'm sure that's very comforting to his family."

"Please, Michael," Jessica said desperately. "It's the only way out of this. They can give you a new identity. They can keep you safe."

"I gotta go."

Jessica stood up quickly. "Don't go, Michael, please! Tell me where you are!" Her plea went unanswered, and she realized he had hung up. She turned to Dominic, who was already talking on his own cell phone. He finished his call and gave her the thumbs up sign.

"You did great. We got a fix on his location. Jake and Chris are heading that way and should be there in five minutes or less."

Jessica grabbed her purse and moved toward the door. "Let's go."

Dominic moved to block her path. "We're staying here. I already got you shot once today. I'm not taking any more chances."

Jessica glared at him. Upset about everything her brother had just revealed, she didn't need this static from Dominic as well. "It's not up to you. We had a deal, remember? I help you out, and you let me be there when he is arrested. It's not my fault a hit man showed up at the bagel shop, and it's certainly not your fault that I got shot."

Dominic crossed his arms and narrowed his eyes. "The deal was, you help us out, and I would do my best to keep Michael alive. That's all there was to it. It's not safe for you to be involved with the arrest. Too many things can go wrong. If you need proof about what I'm saying, just look at your arm." He motioned to her bandages. "Why don't you take a seat and watch a little TV?"

Jessica stiffened her spine and squared her shoulders. "Watch a little TV? You're kidding, right? The last thing I want to do right now is watch TV. Your cohorts are on their way to arrest my brother, and I need to be there, not here. If you'll remember, I was the one who got shot, after all. It's my right to assess the risks and choose whether or not I want to accept them. If I want to be target practice for the bad guys, that's my business, not yours."

Jessica knew her body language and tone of voice made it perfectly clear that her emotions were running high. It probably wasn't the best way to prove that she was calm and rational enough to make this decision for herself, but she'd had just about enough of this man's bossy know-it-all attitude. She glanced around the room again as if searching for something she could throw at him. Something heavy.

"Look, *Mr. U.S. Deputy Marshal.* You wouldn't even know where to look for my brother without my help.

Believe it or not, Michael still trusts me, and he apparently doesn't trust you. If I'm there, it could make the difference between him turning himself in peacefully or someone getting hurt."

Dominic moved toward her until he was only inches away and leaned in. He towered over her, once again using his height to his fullest advantage. "You're forgetting that the marshals involved are trained professionals. Together we've been involved in hundreds of arrests, and we don't need help from a civilian. I let you talk me into allowing you to go to the bagel shop since our back was against the wall, but that was a mistake on my part. I'm not going to make the same mistake twice."

"If I'm there, maybe he'll turn himself in without a fight."

"And maybe he won't. He didn't sound too all-fire cooperative on the phone just now. You could get hurt. Again. In case you don't remember, your safety is my priority. Until I know you're safe, you're not leaving the marshals' custody."

"Oh, yes, I am! I'm done being the bait for you. I'll take my chances on my own." She glared at him and headed for the door, but Dominic wasn't backing down, and he wasn't moving out of the way either. He was big and strong and looked absolutely magnificent as he put his hands on his hips and set his jaw, completely blocking the only door that led out of the room. A hint of attraction swept over her, and she gritted her teeth. The last thing she wanted was to be attracted to this tall, bullheaded deputy; especially now when he was pushing all of her buttons. The anger bristled inside of her, both at Dominic and at herself for the misguided feelings that were springing up in her heart.

Dominic could feel the sparks of attraction as well and was actually surprised at the sensation. He had been around plenty of pretty women before without feeling the draw he was feeling toward the blond firecracker before him. What was so different about Jessica? Maybe it was the unwavering devotion and loyalty she had for her brother, whether he was deserving or not. Or maybe it was the way she took problems in stride and kept pushing forward. Either way, she was an impressive force to be reckoned with, that was for sure.

He ran his fingers through his hair and let out a breath, trying to figure out a way to calm her down. But regardless of his growing feelings for her, there was no way she was leaving this room. She didn't seem to understand that dealing with Ross Kelley and his men could very well be a matter of life and death, even though she had sixteen stitches on her arm to prove it. They were ruthless and didn't seem to care who got hurt along their road to riches. He wasn't about to let her do something stupid like try to go it alone, no matter how much he admired her and her feisty attitude. "You're not going anywhere, Ms. Blake. Please, sit down and wait. As soon as your brother is in custody, I'll arrange for you to see him."

Jessica crossed her arms, and her nostrils flared as she let out a deep breath. Her eyes darted quickly around the room as if she were searching for any possible means of escape. Finding nothing to divert him, she put her hands on her hips and glared at him. "You can't make me stay!" she said defiantly.

"Actually, I can," he said quietly, hoping that his softer tone would settle her down. He was silently thankful for her gaze that revealed the turmoil inside her, because at least that way he could prepare himself and be on guard. He could see her mind working, sifting through possibilities and the odds of escaping him. There was absolutely no way she could overpower him, but he knew that desperate people sometimes tried crazy things that ended up getting someone hurt. He stood motionless but watching, ready for whatever she chose to do next.

"And just how do you plan to do that?"

"You're a material witness in protective custody," Dominic explained coolly. "And if I have to, I'll handcuff you to that chair you were sitting in."

Jessica gasped and took a step back, true astonishment on her face. "You wouldn't dare."

He hoped she could tell from his expression that he would have no qualms at all about following through with his threat. He wasn't backing down on this one. Not when her safety—maybe even her life—were at risk. All traces of the gentlemanly deputy were gone, replaced by a stalwart professional doing his job. Clearly infuriated, she marched up to him, put both hands against his chest and pushed with all her might. She was no match for his strength, however, and he didn't budge an inch. She balled her hands into fists, but he grabbed both of them with his hands and held them tightly before she could strike. He wasn't hurting her, but she was stuck in his grasp like a fly in a spider web.

"Let go of me!" she said, frustrated, her eyes flashing.

He slowly pushed her struggling body back a step at a time until she was backed up against the hotel wall. When she moved to kick him he blocked her with his leg. "You need to settle down," he said quietly.

His face was mere inches from hers, and he noticed the flush in her cheeks and her breath coming in deep, uneven gasps. He thought he could even feel the adrenaline pumping through her body. He knew she was just reacting to the emotional upheaval she'd been through the last few days, but he didn't want anyone getting hurt, and he wasn't sure just what she was capable of doing right now or how far she would go to make her point.

"You promised me you'd let me help," she said bitterly, giving a last futile yank against his grip.

"No, I didn't," Dominic answered quietly. "I promised you I would do everything in my power to help keep Michael alive. There's a big difference."

Jessica blew out a long breath, changing tactics. "You need to let go of me, *Deputy Sullivan*." She said his name slowly and succinctly, her voice rising. "If you think you can manhandle me like this and get away with it, you've got another thing coming. I don't…"

He stopped her flow of words with his lips coming down and covering hers.

She didn't respond at first, but then she suddenly seemed to melt against him. He released her hands and moved back, not breaking the kiss. She took a step forward to stay with him. It was a wonderful kiss, full of warmth and promise, and it sent tingles from her finger-tips to her toes. All of her anger was instantly forgotten, and all she could think about was the sweetness of his lips and the softness of his fingers as he gently cupped her face.

But then Dominic pulled his head away. "What am I doing?" He took several steps back this time until he was five or six feet away from her but still blocking her exit from the room. His hands were back on his hips again, but the look in his eyes had changed to an unreadable blaze. "I'm sorry. That was way out of line...."

Jessica brought her hand to her lips, still tasting his kiss. "It was my fault," she said softly as if talking to herself. "This day has been insane. A few days ago I was just living a normal, quiet life. Today everything is upside down. I'm being shot at, my brother is wanted by the feds, and I just got the most amazing kiss I've ever had. Who would have thought?"

Dominic raised an eyebrow at her comment but let it pass without a comment of his own. Did he disagree? Maybe the kiss that had been so amazing for her had been nothing special for him. Was that why he'd pulled away? He looked uncomfortable now, and embarrassed, which had Jessica feeling self-conscious, as well. Were things going to be awkward between them now? Would the maybe-not-so-wonderful-after-all kiss get in the way of their goals to find her brother and bring him in safely?

And the other question of the hour—who was going to break the increasingly uncomfortable silence?

Finally Dominic motioned toward the chair. "Please sit down, Ms. Blake."

His cell phone rang, and he turned slightly and pushed the receive button, then spoke, apparently relieved at having the distraction. "Sullivan." He listened intently for several seconds, then said, "I understand," and hung up. He turned back to Jessica.

"That was Jake. They were able to nail down Michael's location from your call, but while we were here discussing it, he escaped again. Apparently your brother likes disguises. They saw a cable guy leaving just as they were arriving, but it looked so innocuous they didn't stop him. Of course, the cable company has no record of anyone getting a service call on that street today, so it must have been him. They were able to recover a pay stub from a downtown restaurant at the house where he was staying, however. Jake is trying to run it down right now to see if it belonged to Michael or not. It's not in his name, but Michael might be using a false identity. He probably needs the money since he cleared out of Atlanta so quickly."

Jessica sat down wearily, the relief that there hadn't been a showdown making her knees weak. She rubbed her abdomen absently. "I'm so worried about him my stomach hurts," she said quietly, then jumped back up and turned to Dominic as a new thought hit her. "I'm going to have to call him again. I just hope he trusts me enough to still talk to me. Do you think he saw the marshals when they tried to arrest him just now?"

Dominic shrugged. "There's no telling."

Jessica nodded in response, then sat down heavily once more, feeling a little like a yo-yo.

She looked at Dominic. His jaw was set in determination, yet there was still a boyish quality to his features that made him approachable and appealing. She was attracted to his strength, despite his obstinacy, and at this moment wanted nothing more than to have him hold her and hear him say that everything was going to be okay. She had known loneliness many times in her life, but she could never remember feeling it as acutely as she did now. What would she do if she lost Michael?

She remembered the pain she had felt when her parents had died. It had been almost debilitating, especially at her young age, and she never wanted to feel that depth of pain again. It was much easier to push people away and keep her heart protected, and she had done a pretty good job of keeping herself safe from that type of pain during most of her life. If she didn't get too close, she couldn't get hurt. But it was different with Michael. Even though her brother had pulled away from her and was involved with something she didn't understand, she still loved him with her whole heart. How could she go on if she lost the only family she had left? She took a deep breath and gritted her teeth as a new wave of determination swept over her.

She would be strong, and with God's help, she would make it through this. She said a short prayer for perseverance, then returned again to Dominic, another question on the tip of her tongue.

At the same moment, bullets sprayed across the room, sending shards of plaster and glass spewing all over the floor and furniture.

SEVEN

Dominic grabbed Jessica and pulled her to the floor behind the bed, just missing the barrage of bullets and plaster. He shielded her with his body, waiting for the submachine gun fire to end. The noise was deafening, like finding yourself at ground zero for the detonation of some kind of bomb. She huddled beneath Dominic, terrified. The bullets stopped as suddenly as they had begun, and tires squealed out in the parking lot in the ensuing silence. Dominic waited a full two minutes, then looked at Jessica who was still trembling beneath him.

"Are you all right?" He rolled slowly away from her, noticing the whiteness of her skin. Her big blue eyes were as round as saucers, and her whole body seemed to be shaking. He ran his hands up her arms, looking for blood or other injuries. They were both covered in bits of plaster and dust, but he didn't find any wounds.

"No new bullet holes, if that's what you mean," she whispered in a brittle voice. His hands had settled on her wrists, and he could feel her pulse beating like a snare drum in a parade. She pulled her hands out of his grip and tried to brush the dust out of her eyes, but she was shaking so badly she couldn't quite manage it. She started to get up, but he gently pushed her back down.

"Stay down and behind the bed while I check this out." He started to move toward the shattered window, but Jessica grabbed his shirt and stopped him.

"Please, be careful," she whispered, her voice tight.

He met her eyes and saw worry and fear mirrored back at him. He smiled reassuringly at her and gave her hand a squeeze as she released his shirt. Then he moved cautiously toward the broken front window and looked past the curtains that were now shredded from the gunfire. The gunman was no longer in the parking lot, but the curious would soon appear and the shooter could always return. They needed to get out of there. Fast. He called back to Jessica.

"They're gone. Let's move. Grab your bag, or what's left of it, and let's go."

He moved toward the door, but when he glanced back at her, he noted that she still hadn't moved. He returned to her side with catlike swiftness and gently brushed her hair out of her eyes, sensing her distress. He gave her another smile. "Take a deep breath. Yes, that's right. Okay. Let's get you to your feet." He gently slid his hands under her arms and helped her stand up. Then he pulled her into his arms and held her for a moment. She was soft and sweet and seemed to just melt against him. She also fit perfectly as if they were made for each other. He couldn't help but think back to the kiss they'd shared only minutes before. It really *had* been amazing, even if he had absolutely no business letting it happen. Jessica was a witness in his custody. There was no way he could do his job properly and keep her safe if his emotions got involved. He had to fight this attraction. That was all there was to it. But right now, in this moment, was it really so wrong to offer a little comfort? He could feel her heart beating against his chest, and he rubbed her back gently. They stood together for a moment longer, then Dominic pulled away.

"I could stay here like this all afternoon, but it's not safe. We need to get out of here before that shooter comes back and tries to finish the job."

She nodded, finally getting herself back under control. She glanced around the room, found her bag and slung it over her shoulder. It had a small tear in the strap, but had otherwise survived the shooting unscathed. "Sorry. I'm good now. Let's get out of here." She straightened, then followed him out the door and down to the car. A few people were sticking their heads out the doors, wondering about the gunfire they had heard, but no one got in their way. Dominic escorted Jessica to the car, then drove out of the parking lot. They made a few quick turns to make sure they weren't being followed, then pulled over into another parking lot with a dark green Dumpster in the corner next to an old empty office building that had a large "for rent" sign in the front window. The location was perfect for what he had in mind. Dominic put the car in park and turned to Jessica.

"Do you have your cell phone with you?"

"Sure," Jessica nodded. She reached into her bag and pulled out the phone.

"Okay. Write down any phone numbers you might need, erase them and then I'm going to toss it. We were tracking Michael by his cell phone. It's a good bet that Coastal is tracking us by yours." That was one theory. He was afraid to even mention the other fears that were pelting his brain. He didn't believe in coincidences. Someone from the inside had to be feeding information to Coastal.

"But how could they know the number?"

Dominic drew his lips into a thin line. He wasn't ready to tell her his thoughts on that subject. For now it was enough to assuage her fear. "Coastal has almost unlimited resources. A cell phone number is a very small problem. And we've had your phone on constantly while we were waiting for a call from Michael. I should have thought of it before. That was a costly mistake on my part. One I won't make again." He watched her pull out her cell and nodded. "After you copy down your phone book, call and leave Michael a message. Tell him you're having trouble with your cell phone and you're going to be calling him from a different number." He could tell she was hesitating, and his eyes met hers. "You've been shot at twice today. We don't want them to try a third time."

She paused a moment more, then wrote down a few numbers, left Michael a message and handed the phone over to Dominic, her hand trembling. Dominic took the phone, made sure it was turned on and threw it in the Dumpster. Then they were back on the road again. Once they hit the city limits, Dominic pulled over to a gas station and bought a prepaid cell phone with cash. He left Jessica in the car while he walked a few feet away toward a pay phone and called Jake. He had to trust someone. Jake was his closest friend in law enforcement and could also guarantee a secure phone line.

Jake's voice was upbeat when he answered. "Jake Riley."

"It's Dominic, Jake. Make sure you have a secure line and give me a call back at this number." He fed him the number from his new cell phone and hung up. A moment later, the new cell was ringing.

"Jake?"

"What's happening, Dominic?"

He told Jake briefly what had happened, then told him what he had done with Jessica's phone and asked him to set up surveillance of the Dumpster and the surrounding area. Sooner or later, someone would come looking for that phone, and his gut told him it would be someone on Coastal's payroll.

"We've got a problem, Jake. Levine's death, the bagel shop hit and now the hotel? There's no way this is all just a coincidence. We've got a leak somewhere, and this last security breach proves it. Somebody has to be dirty. Someone we trust on the task force."

Jake blew out a breath. "I don't want to believe it, but I don't believe in coincidences, either. What's your next move?"

"My brothers have an associate in their law firm named Chris Hamilton. He owns a river house on the Ochlockonee that he rarely uses, and I'm sure he won't care if we hole up there for a few days. I doubt anyone at Coastal will make the connection, so we should be safe, at least for a while. I'm taking Jessica there now. We can reconvene once we have a better handle on this. No more communication through normal channels. No more sharing intel with the task force until we can get a handle on this. Sound good to you?"

"Yeah. That's the way it's gotta be. I'll make sure I get a secure phone with no ties to the task force, then call you after you get settled. Not a word to anyone but me. I'll also start doing some checking. Hopefully our perp left some sort of trail."

"Thanks, Jake." He flipped the phone closed, then returned to the car and Jessica, who was anxiously waiting for him with fear still in her eyes.

"Where are we going?"

Dominic gave her a reassuring smile and squeezed her hand. "To a new safe house. I'm not having trouble convincing anyone that your life is in danger, and the rest of our plans haven't changed. We need to regroup."

"Is someone going to explain to the police what happened at the hotel?"

"Sure, one of the marshals will take care of it." He grimaced. "Someone must have paid extremely well to find out what room we were in. They'll follow up on that, too."

They were several miles down the road before Jessica spoke again. "Do you have any family, Marshal?"

Dominic glanced in her direction, then turned his eyes back on the road. Part of him wished she'd call him by his given name, but if that happened, it would be even harder to maintain distance in their relationship.

"Marshal" would have to do for now. "I have two older brothers and an amazing mom."

Jessica mulled over the information. She remembered he'd mentioned his father had died. She also noticed he didn't list a girlfriend or a wife, and she was pretty sure the man would never have kissed her if he were married or even dating someone. He was a straight arrow. It showed in his mannerisms and the way he spoke. It was also one more reason why she liked him so much. "Do you have a good relationship with your brothers?"

Dominic smiled. "We have a great relationship. We're a very close family and we usually see each other once a week or more, if I'm not working a case." He saw her surprised expression out of the corner of his eye. "Both of my brothers went to law school at Florida State and still live here in Tallahassee. We also all go to the same church, so we see each other there during the services. On Sunday afternoons, we usually get together for a big meal at my mother's house. It's pretty much become a tradition. She loves to cook and always has a huge spread of southern favorites on the table. It's like a weekly family reunion." He paused. "Have you heard of Sullivan and Sullivan, the law firm here in town?"

Jessica's eyes widened. "Sure. They helped out a friend of mine in a property dispute."

"Well, those are my brothers, Alex and Ryan Sullivan."

Jessica laughed. Dominic wasn't sure what was so funny, but he was pleased to see that the change in topic had taken her mind off her current troubles. "It sure is a small world. I've never seen them advertise on TV or anything, but I actually remember that they sponsored a city league baseball team for some of my students. My kids had 'Sullivan and Sullivan' written on the back of their jerseys, and they wore them to school every time they had a game."

It was Dominic's turn to laugh. "That would be due to Alex. He was one of the stars on the Florida State baseball team during college and was on his way up to the majors as a pitcher before he injured his arm. He loves baseball."

"Well, the kids sure appreciated it. Apparently the law firm even bought the trophies for the team at the end of the season and had a huge pizza party for the awards ceremony." She eyed him speculatively. "Why aren't you a lawyer, too?"

Dominic shrugged, feeling almost sheepish. "I was never the serious student like my brothers were. I spent most of my younger years getting into trouble and having them bail me out of it."

Jessica raised an eyebrow. "What kind of trouble?" she asked, looking every inch the schoolteacher.

Dominic laughed at her serious expression. "Not legal trouble, if that's what you're thinking. I, ah…" he coughed to hide his embarrassment. "I had a habit of playing practical jokes on people. Some of them were classics. Others didn't work out so well."

He was pleased when Jessica smiled. This was a side of him that he rarely showed anymore. He was glad she seemed to appreciate it. "Oh, really? Sounds like you've got some great stories to tell."

"Yeah, well…" He grinned back at her. "My favorite

was back in college when we 'borrowed' all of the toilet seats from the top two floors of my dorm and used them to decorate the university president's front lawn. The president was, ah, shall we say, less than pleased?"

Jessica broke out laughing. "Did they find out it was you?"

"Nope. That's still the best-kept secret of my freshman year. Shh." He put his finger on his lips. "Don't tell anyone. The president still thinks some crazy fraternity is to blame."

Jessica nodded solemnly, then broke out laughing again. "Your secret's safe with me." She gave him a smile. "Tell me another one."

Dominic returned the smile. "Well, once when I was a sophomore, I got an empty salt shaker and filled it about half way up with lemon juice. Then I attached a little pocket of tissue paper under the lid that was filled with baking soda and put it on the table at the dining hall. Another guy picked it up and started shaking it pretty hard because nothing would come out. That made the lemon juice and baking soda mix together, and when that happened, the lid blew off and foam went everywhere. It was a great gag."

Jessica was really laughing now. "Nobody got mad?"

Dominic shook his head. "Nah. I had to watch my back for a few days, just in case he decided to retaliate, but it was just a bunch of guys having fun."

Jessica let out a happy sigh. Slowly she reached over and grasped Dominic's hand, then leaned back against the seat and closed her eyes. He knew he should pull away from the contact, but he allowed it and even rubbed his thumb gently over the back of her hand. They said little else during the rest of the trip. A peaceful feeling enveloped Dominic as he drove along, holding her hand while she dozed. He was glad she felt comfortable enough to sleep so easily, even after all she'd been through in the past few days—trusting him to keep her safe as she slept.

Dear God, please don't let me fail.

"It didn't happen? How is that possible?" The entire desk shook violently as Kelley pounded it with his fists in frustration. Pens and folders filled with documents went flying as he swept them from the surface. Even the vein in his forehead pulsed with anger, and spittle formed at the corner of his mouth. "I paid good money for their location. Was the information we received erroneous?"

Martin held up his hands in mock surrender and took a step backwards. He knew better than to do or say anything that would fuel his boss's rage. "No, the location was correct. The shooter attempted the hit, but he failed to verify the kill."

Kelley narrowed his eyes. He didn't tolerate incompetence and *failure* wasn't an option. "What kind of people are you hiring—teenagers straight out of juvenile detention?"

"No, sir, but apparently professionals in Tallahassee that guarantee their work are few and far between." He straightened his shoulders. "I'm just as frustrated as you are, Mr. Kelley, but I have a proposition."

Kelley sat back down in his chair and eyed Martin speculatively. "I'm listening."

"With your permission, I'll go to Tallahassee myself and take care of this problem personally."

Kelley raised an eyebrow as he considered Martin's words. He was clearly surprised by the offer. "Are you sure? I mean, I know you're qualified, but…"

"I did a tour with the military right out of college," Martin said quietly, "and I've kept current with my weapons training. I can handle the job."

Kelley paused a moment longer, then leaned forward and announced his conclusion. "Book the next flight out. I want this problem fixed and I want it fixed now."

Martin nodded, both relieved and determined. "Understood. Like I said, I'll take care of it personally."

EIGHT

The new safe house was actually a house this time instead of a hotel room and was at the end of an old dirt road that paralleled the river. The structure wasn't much to look at and seemed more like an old fishing shack than a habitable building. But it was secluded and surrounded by two acres of land filled with pine trees and scrub oaks on three sides and the Ochlockonee River on the other, Dominic had told her driving in. The inside of the house was actually cleaner than she expected, and the furniture could only be described as being a hodgepodge of different styles and colors. The common theme seemed to be comfort, however, and Jessica was actually looking forward to a soft mattress and a few hours of uninterrupted sleep. She was given a quick tour of the house, then found a bundle of unopened personal supplies in the bathroom and did her nightly rituals of braiding her hair, brushing her teeth and taking a long, hot shower.

She felt like she was nearly sleepwalking when she entered the hallway a half hour later, but Dominic stopped her just as she was heading to the smaller of the two bedrooms. His expression was grim and made her feel as if all of the camaraderie that they had shared on the ride to the safe house had been erased. When he spoke, his voice was deadly serious and his steel gray eyes were filled with intensity.

"Are you going to try to go it alone again, or can I trust you to stay put?"

She looked up at him and blew out a breath. Although she was a strong woman, she had been through an awful lot the last couple of days, and she knew the weariness showed in the strain around her eyes and mouth. Even so, she still managed to summon a spark of defiance. She shrugged nonchalantly, even though indifference was really the last thing she was feeling. "That depends. What's your plan?"

Dominic gently reached out, took hold of her hand and gave it a gentle squeeze, yet the intensity in his eyes didn't waver. "We're not sure yet. Jake just got here, and we're going to discuss our options. The pay stub they found was for a John Clark. Do you recognize the name?"

Jessica nodded faintly, a little unnerved by Dominic's tough cop exterior coupled with his caring gestures. "John was a friend of Michael's back in high school. He died in a freak boating accident out in the gulf during a fishing trip."

Dominic locked her eyes with his own, probing, but this time he almost seemed to be pleading with her as well. The caring she saw in his gaze sent a tingle down her spine.

"You didn't answer my question. Will you give me your word that you'll stay?"

Jessica raised an eyebrow and tried to stay focused. "My word is enough for you?"

Dominic grinned in response and squeezed her hand. "You bet. If you can't trust a teacher, who can you trust?"

Jessica was pleased by his answer, and his grin did crazy things to her insides. She looked at their hands, linked together, then back into the warm expression of the man before her. Although she had been frustrated and angry earlier, down deep she knew that her best chance of helping Michael and keeping herself alive lay in the hands of the U.S. Marshals.

"I'll stay."

Dominic raised her hand to his lips and kissed it gently, and she could see the mixture of relief and gratitude in his expression. "Thanks. I'll walk you back and let you get some rest now."

Jake was in the living room setting up some electronic equipment when they walked in. He noticed their linked hands, and how they quickly let go when they entered the room. He looked pointedly at Dominic and raised an eyebrow. Dominic shook his head and let out a breath, knowing they would discuss this later but not wanting to have this conversation in front of Jessica. He had stepped over the line again. He knew it, and now Jake knew it, too.

Jake cleared his throat. "The manager confirmed that this guy Clark has only been working at the restaurant for a few days. He gave us a description that didn't match Blake exactly, but it could be that Michael is using another one of his disguises. The address the guy gave on his application was fake, as well as the social security number. Clark is on the schedule to show up tomorrow at ten in the morning, so our best bet is to be there waiting for him when he walks in and see for ourselves if he's our man."

Dominic looked at Jessica and watched determination replace the exhaustion in a matter of seconds. When she spoke, her voice was tough and gritty. "Don't even think of leaving me behind. I'm going."

Dominic put his hands up in mock surrender. "Whoa. One thing at a time. I'm not looking to fight about this. We haven't even decided on a course of action yet. Do we have to discuss your involvement right off the bat?"

Jessica narrowed her eyes, her expression clearly indicating that his response was not the one she was hoping for. "If your answer isn't immediately 'yes', then I guess we do."

Dominic hesitated as he watched the anger sweep across Jessica's face. He had no intention of including her in the arrest scenario, but he hadn't thought ahead to how he could appease her either. His mind whirled. There had to be a way to make her understand that she needed to stay at the safe house while they conducted the arrest without her, but if getting shot at hadn't convinced her to stay out of the line of fire, what would?

"Don't start getting upset," he said quietly, trying to pacify her. "We don't do anything without a plan. We'll make the decision about who goes and who stays once we check out this restaurant and get a lay of the land." Dominic could tell by her expression that she wasn't buying it, and he felt a wave of insecurity go down his spine. He'd only known this woman for a few short days, but she was amazing, and her fortitude off the charts. He should have known this battle was coming and planned accordingly. He shook his head and mentally kicked himself for his lack of foresight. When she put her hands on her hips, he answered by taking an intimidating step in her direction. "You gave me your word, Jessica. Remember?"

"I take it back," she said vehemently, unaffected by his stance. "Don't you understand yet that you need me?"

Jake looked from the determined eyes of Jessica into the frustrated eyes of Dominic. He stood and backed out of the room. It was obvious that he didn't want to be anywhere nearby when this bomb exploded. "Time for a snack. I'll be in the kitchen if you need me."

"Coward," Dominic muttered under his breath. He watched Jake go, then turned back to Jessica who had now crossed her arms and was staring him down. He knew that if he didn't say what she wanted to hear, he would have to watch her every minute to make sure she didn't try to disappear to help Michael on her own, despite her exhausted condition. Still, he couldn't bring himself to promise she could come when they attempted to arrest her brother. She had already been shot at twice and had a knot on her head and stitches in her arm, all thanks to Coastal. Didn't she see the dangers? The marshals had been trained in fugitive apprehension, and now they had the leak to consider, which was no small problem. In fact, the leak made everything they did more dangerous by two. Jessica was an elementary schoolteacher. She had been trained in how to teach a child the ABCs and multiplication tables. How could he justify putting her life in danger one more time? He would never be able to forgive himself if she got hurt again on his watch. He would also rather cuff her to a chair than lie to her.

"Look, Jessica, I'm listening to you, and I've heard everything you've said, but I can't promise anything yet. Give us some time to work out a plan and talk through our options. Okay?"

Her glance darted around behind him, and Dominic knew she was weighing the chances of getting by him and getting out the door. He put up his hands in mock surrender again and shook his head. "Jessica, don't do it. Don't even try. *Please.* I'm a really big guy, and you're not going to get by me, not to mention Jake in the other room. You'll never make it out of the house, and I have the car keys, which means even if you did get out of the building, you'd be on foot and an easy target. Think of your safety. After the hotel and the bagel shop, you know they're gunning for you."

"I can't think about that right now," she answered defiantly. "All I care about is finding Michael and working out a way to save his life. If you're not going to let me help, then I'll just have to find a way to do it on my own." She took a step toward the door and he quickly took a step to the left and blocked her path. She swiftly took a step to the right in response, and again, he moved to block her.

"You're not leaving here, Jessica. Get that through your head right here and right now."

"You can't make me stay," she said rebelliously. "Somehow I'll find him and make sure he's safe. Then we'll figure a way out of this mess."

"It's too late to change the game plan now," he said firmly, his tone leaving no room for argument. "You're here and you'll stay here. Can't you see that I'm trying to keep *you* safe? Coastal wants you dead! I'm trying to keep you alive."

Jessica glared at him, her body tense and ready for motion, but Dominic held his ground. He knew she had to realize on some level that he was right and she was no match for him physically. She also had to know that it would be foolish for her to even try, yet emotionally she had been on a giant roller coaster, and he knew from experience that people under stress didn't always do the smartest things.

"Don't make me cuff you," Dominic threatened softly, although he really didn't see how he could avoid doing just that if she was bound and determined to escape him. He read the emotions as they flitted across her face, and he knew that he was in trouble. Even if she backed down now, Jessica Blake was going to try to make a run for it before the night was through, despite her physical and emotional exhaustion. It was written all over her face. And that was one thing he couldn't allow to happen.

At some point, he was going to have to rest and get a little shut-eye himself. Neither he nor Jake could watch her constantly, and he could tell by her reactions that he couldn't leave her to her own devices and expect her to still be there when he woke up in the morning. That didn't leave him with many options, and from the look in her eye, he could tell that she knew it.

Jessica took a step forward but he held his ground. Her blue eyes flashed like flames. "Just try cuffing me, Marshal!"

"Haven't we gone through this before?" Talking time was over. He could see very clearly that nothing he said was going to change her mind. He pulled out his handcuffs and before she knew it, he had one of the silver bracelets around her wrist. He lifted her effortlessly, despite her kicking, and carried her back to the smaller of the two bedrooms. Once there, he sat her down on a wooden chair and moved back quickly before her swinging fists could connect with his face.

"Whoa there, lady," he said forcefully. She tried to get up, but he pushed her back down, then grabbed her right wrist that had the cuff and closed the other bracelet around the wooden rung, effectively locking her to the heavy furniture. She squirmed and tried to grab him but the handcuffs and the weight of the chair held her back, and she actually jerked against them as he moved out of reach. Her face registered pain, but it was quickly replaced by outrage.

"Okay, Mr. U.S. Marshal. You win. You're bigger and stronger than I am. But this can't be legal. Where's the key?"

"Out of your range, firecracker. Get a good night's sleep and we'll talk in the morning."

"How am I supposed to sleep when I'm chained here like a dog?"

"You made your choice. Now live with the consequences." He turned to leave but stopped when she called to him. Her voice was still angry, but this time it was also laced with the slightest plea and it nearly undid him. He hadn't wanted to be so rough with her, but she had really left him little choice.

"I'm sorry, Marshal. Really. You don't need to do this."

He stiffened. He couldn't back down now. He had to do whatever it took to keep her safe. "Too little, too late, Ms. Blake. I need to get some sleep myself, and there's no way I can do that if I have to worry about you knocking me out and making a run for it."

"For the record, I wouldn't knock you out."

He noticed she didn't promise to stay put. "Yeah, and pigs are flying outside as we speak."

She leaned back against the chair and jerked against the cuffs in a useless, frustrated gesture. "I can't believe you just handcuffed me to a chair."

"Believe it. I told you before, I'm a man of my word. I'm going to make sure you're safe, even if it means I have to protect you from yourself."

She grimaced. "You know, you've already discovered that Michael's pretty slippery. You need me. You really do. And the Coastal people won't be anywhere around tomorrow because they aren't tracking my cell phone anymore. There's no danger if I go along. None at all."

Dominic shook his head. "We don't know for sure

how the Coastal people got the tip about the bagel shop or how they found us at the hotel, despite my cell phone theories. For all we know, they could have been tracking Michael by his phone or some other method for the first hit, and maybe they found us at the hotel through simple surveillance. There are literally hundreds of ways to track a person, and we can't assume Coastal doesn't know about our plans just because we ditched your phone. When we make assumptions, people get hurt." He kept his thoughts about the leak to himself. At this point, all he had were theories, not cold, hard facts. What he needed was some time to sit down and talk everything out with Jake. Then they would make their plans for the morning. He would not be rushed into making a bad decision, especially when it came to Jessica's welfare. He softened his voice and met her eyes. "I don't want one of those people to be you. I want you safe. Period."

Jessica gritted her teeth. "He's my brother. I should be able to make that choice."

Dominic shrugged. "We haven't decided the best course of action yet. Like I said before, we need a plan. Once Jake and I have a chance to talk, we'll figure out what we're going to do." A small part of him regretted handcuffing her to the chair, but only a small part. He would feel much worse if she got away from them and got herself killed. "Get some sleep. We'll talk in the morning." With that he turned and left, closing the door softly behind him. He took a few steps away and leaned against the wall, then closed his eyes and rubbed his forehead. He could hear her searching through the dresser end table, then banging the drawers closed in frustration. He wasn't sure what she was looking for, but he knew there was nothing in those drawers but old fishing magazines and linens for the bed. He had checked them himself when they first arrived. A few moments later, he heard the mattress springs squeak and he hoped she was settling in for the night. He waited a moment longer, then headed toward the kitchen.

Dominic went straight to the cabinet and got himself a drink of water at the sink. When he turned, he saw Jake watching him carefully as he stirred his coffee in a slow, steady motion.

He had known Jake for about four years now, and had been through a lot with the other man as they had chased fugitives across the state. This was the first time Dominic had ever gotten this close to a witness, however, and he knew, as they all did, that getting personally involved was never a good idea. Once the emotions were engaged, law enforcement officers frequently made mistakes, and mistakes could get someone killed. Jake wasn't the kind of man to report Dominic up the chain of command or ask to have him reassigned, but Dominic could sense that his friend was worried about him and the way that this could all play out.

"That's one unhappy woman," Jake said softly in his deep southern accent.

Dominic glanced up and into the eyes of his friend. There wasn't condemnation there, but there was definitely a question. Dominic knew Jake to be a quiet observer of all he surveyed. Although Jake didn't say a lot, there wasn't much that escaped his attention. Jake had noticed more than just the two of them holding hands.

"Did you lock her in that room?"

Dominic shrugged slightly. "No. There's not much of a lock on that door, and she could have gone out the window if she'd really tried. I handcuffed her to a chair. If I hadn't, she'd be gone already."

Jake whistled in surprise, then laughed. "Boy, you'd better watch your back. She's a spitfire from the word go."

Dominic nodded his agreement and took a deep breath. "She wants to come to the restaurant tomorrow so she can be there for the arrest. She says she won't stay in the safe house unless I promise to let her come."

"Even after she got shot in the arm and almost killed at the hotel?"

"Even so."

Jake paused, considering. "And you don't want her to?"

Dominic ran his hand through his hair and sighed. "I want her safe. The next bullet they fire at her could have her name on it."

"You also want to arrest Michael Blake, and she can help." He put down his cup and picked up some papers that he'd brought with him in a briefcase. "I've been reading up on Blake's background. He was in the drama program in high school and apparently got some training in disguises. He's no professional, but we need to be careful here. He got away from us in the bagel shop and again at his apartment. He's done a pretty good job of staying underground for an amateur, despite Coastal's attempt to flush him out." Jake paused. "He's smarter than we think, and she might be able to help us spot him."

Dominic narrowed his eyes. "What are you saying?"

"I'm saying, don't let your feelings for this lady make you take your eyes off the ball. We're here to arrest Michael Blake. Period. That's our primary objective."

Dominic nodded. "Message received, Jake. Loud and clear."

"Good." He took a sip of his coffee, grimaced, then poured it down the drain. "Nasty stuff," he muttered under his breath. "Didn't you say that the guy who owns this place is a lawyer? You'd figure a guy like that would at least stock it with some decent coffee to make our jobs a little easier."

Dominic smiled, grateful for the change of subject. Jake was a gourmet coffee man and liked the bold, exotic brews that shot caffeine through his system in one giant rush. His disdain for cheap coffee was a nice dose of normalcy. But then Dominic's mind turned to the leak, and he sat down heavily. "Who do we trust, Jake? Who on the task force could be desperate enough to be selling information to Coastal?"

"We trust Chris and Whitney. Period." His expression turned to granite. "The location of this house and our witness don't go beyond our own team—not to the task force or even to the local police. I've got Whitney discreetly doing some research. She's preparing a list of people who could have known enough to sell out Levine and give out the locations of the sites for the two hits today. It won't be a long list. Once she gets that narrowed down, we'll decide on our next move."

Dominic nodded. "If anyone can find them, Whitney can. She's the best researcher I've seen." He stood and opened a few of the cabinets. "Any decent food up here? I'm actually a little hungry."

"Chris is on his way and bringing a pizza. If he knows what's good for him, he'll bring a few caffeine-filled soda pops along too. He called a few minutes ago and said he got a copy of the floor plan for the restaurant and some sort of surveillance video that we can watch to get the lay of the land."

"Sounds good." Dominic leaned against the counter, his stance thoughtful. "Listen, Jake, Michael said something interesting when he called Jessica earlier today. He said he did the counterfeiting because he needed the money. Problem is, I don't remember him living beyond his means in Atlanta, and I also don't remember seeing any large sums in his bank accounts. This counterfeiting has been going on for a while. What happened to his cash?"

Jake shrugged. "That's a good question. His apartment didn't even have a decent TV or stereo system, and he sure wasn't driving anything fancy. I'll check his credit cards and bank statements one more time to see if anything catches my eye. He doesn't have a drug problem, does he?"

"Not that I know of. I never saw any signs of gambling debts, either." He stretched. It had been a very long day, and still wasn't over by a long shot. "Thanks for looking over the statements. I'm going to keep working on the paperwork until Chris gets here." Dominic opened the refrigerator and leaned on the door, but didn't see anything that interested him. He shrugged and shut the door, then returned to the computer in the living room where he was writing up his latest report.

Chris arrived a few minutes later, and the three men ate as they planned. At one point, Dominic took a slice of pizza back to Jessica to give her as a peace offering, but she had pulled the chair over to lie down on the bed and was fast asleep. She didn't rouse when he opened the door so he took a moment and just watched her sleep. The last few days had been hard on her, but even with her tired features she looked simply beautiful to Dominic. He admired her determination, despite the trouble she was giving him. He thought back to the kiss they had shared and smiled. She was a very special lady. He wanted to protect her...but Jake was right. His assignment here was to arrest Michael Blake. He had to keep his focus. He'd be no good to anyone if he continued on his present course. He needed detachment. He needed to ignore his attraction to this feisty lady and concentrate on doing his job. Then, maybe once this case was over and he was no longer involved with her in a professional capacity, he could explore these feelings that were constantly keeping her in his thoughts and making his heart beat a little faster anytime she was around him.

Dominic had been immature when he had started with the Marshal's office, but had worked long and hard to get rid of his joker image and be taken seriously as a law enforcement officer. He was now doing extremely well in his career, and he didn't need to stumble now that he had established himself and was on a successful track.

Dear Lord, please keep her safe. I don't want to screw this up and make a mistake. Help me make wise decisions and keep my emotions in check so I can do my job effectively without someone getting hurt.

He leaned back in the chair and closed his eyes, concentrating. Focus. It was all about focus, and tomorrow the focus would be on arresting Michael Blake.

NINE

Jessica woke up with a start, and it took her a full minute to realize where she was. She'd been dreaming about… She grimaced. She'd been dreaming about Dominic! She was horrified. She couldn't remember a man ever making her so mad, and now she was even dreaming about him! Ugh! In the dream someone had been chasing her with a gun, and Dominic was trying to save her. They were running through a forest and she was getting so tired, even though the danger was getting closer and closer.….She shook her head as if to clear the images from her mind. The last thing she needed was Dominic Sullivan even more firmly implanted in her mind. She rolled but was stopped by the handcuff. She jerked against the hard metal and was instantly sorry. Her wrist was already sore, and now pinpricks of pain were shooting up her arm. She rubbed her wrist absently, thinking about the events of the evening before. She had been livid that Dominic refused to see why she needed to be involved in Michael's arrest, yet at the same time, a small part of her was also relieved that the marshal had stopped her from making a potentially dangerous decision. She had been stressed and tired, but now after a few hours of sleep she saw the situation more clearly.

She lay still and listened for a moment, wondering if anyone else was still in the house. She didn't hear a thing. Could they have already left for the hotel to arrest Michael?

"Hey!" she called. "Is anybody out there?" She looked around the room. The thick curtains made it difficult to know what time it was, but a small sliver of pale sunlight made her guess that it was still pretty early in the morning. "Hey!" she called again. "Anybody home?"

She wished there was something she could throw against the door to make some noise, but the room was devoid of knickknacks. Because of the way the furniture was situated, she also couldn't pull the chair she was handcuffed to close enough to the door to bang on it with her fist. She sat for a minute, considering, then finally pulled out the small drawer in the end table, took out the magazines that she found inside and maneuvered the drawer out of the runners. It was only about as big as a shoe box, but it would probably make some racket on impact. She slung it at the door at exactly the same time that someone else started to open it.

"Whoa!" Dominic closed the door quickly. After a pause, he slowly opened the door again. He peeked around the edge, looking for other possible projectiles that she might be ready to throw at his head. She sat on the edge of the chair trying to appear sweet and innocent. She watched him look at the hand that was locked to the rung of the chair, and he grimaced when he couldn't see the other one. "Let me see your other hand, Jessica."

She couldn't resist teasing him and gave him an innocent smile as she exaggerated her southern accent. "Are you worried about little ole me, Marshal? Remember, you're much bigger and stronger than I am. I couldn't possibly cause you any trouble."

"Your hand, Jessica." His voice was firm, but his lip twitched.

She slowly lifted her other hand, palm up. It was empty.

He opened the door further, but still seemed a little wary.

"You didn't leave me anything else to throw, Marshal. And I had to get your attention somehow." She smiled sheepishly. "I really need to go to the bathroom."

He nodded, approached her cautiously and bent over to unlock the cuffs.

Once she was free, she stretched out her arm and rubbed her wrist. "Thanks." She moved away from him and headed for the bathroom, closing the door behind her. After taking care of business, she left the water running in the sink while she searched through the cabinets, looking for anything that might be useful if the marshals resorted to locking her up to keep her away from her brother again. A knock on the door startled her, and she dropped a tube of toothpaste she had found in the drawer.

"Finish up, Jessica. We need to talk."

She sighed and turned off the water. There were only

a few toiletry items in the cabinet, and nothing that would be of any use. Dominic and Jake were more than she could handle anyway, and deep down she knew it. She didn't have it in her to hurt them, and she was no match for them physically. She looked for a window, but there was only a small one over the shower that was much too tiny for her to fit through, and the house was on stilts over the water, so the drop would be long, and the landing, from this side of the house, would be wet. She sighed, dried her hands, and left the bathroom. Her best bet and only real choice was to use her brain and convince them that they should take her with them to the restaurant. Maybe now after she'd had some sleep, she could behave more rationally and use logic to win her case, pure and simple.

Dominic was waiting for her when she emerged and was sitting uncomfortably in the wooden chair. The handcuffs were nowhere in sight, and he motioned for her to sit on the bed. She obeyed but she stayed tense and held herself stiffly.

Dominic opened a folder he was holding and pulled out an eight-by-ten glossy photograph. It showed a man wearing sunglasses behind the wheel of a car. The man had dark hair, tanned skin and a rather large nose. Jessica raised an eyebrow.

"Who's he?"

"That is Jeff Martin, one of the top dogs at Coastal. He was indicted for the counterfeiting along with your brother, and we think he was also involved in killing another witness." He put the photo back in the folder and closed it, then set it aside. "That picture was taken yesterday. Remember when I threw your cell phone away in that Dumpster? Well Mr. Martin was seen at that same location a few hours later, scoping out the scene. We think that Kelley got a little miffed when his first two attempts on your life failed, so now he's sending in someone he can trust to do the job right. If you had any doubts that they were following your cell phone trail, throw them out the window. This photo confirms they were tracking you."

Jessica's face paled a little, and she rubbed her hands together nervously. "So, you were right."

"Yeah, it certainly looks that way. I wasn't joking when I said these guys were dangerous, either. We think Martin is still in town, and make no mistake, he's gunning for you, and he wants you dead. He's not some shooter for hire. He's got a real stake in eliminating you and Michael." He paused, locking eyes with Jessica. It was obvious he didn't want to say anything more, but he pressed forward. "There's something else you should know. We think we have a leak—someone in law enforcement who is giving Coastal information about you. That's why I brought you all the way out here. Right now only the marshal team knows that you're here, and we're going to keep it that way. From this point forward, don't trust anyone but the four of us. Not the local police, not the FBI. No one. Do you understand?"

Jessica nodded solemnly. It was hard to believe that someone in law enforcement would be working in league with Coastal, yet in this day and age, anything seemed possible.

"We decided on our plan last night."

Jessica sat a little taller, her face eager, despite what Dominic had just revealed. "And?"

Dominic sighed. "And against my better judgment, we've decided to let you come with us for the arrest."

"Thank you!" She jumped up and gave him a rambunctious hug, pleased that she hadn't had to argue with him any further and that he had finally seen the light.

"Whoa," he said, laughing as she nearly knocked him out of the chair. "Does this mean you've forgiven me for the handcuffs?" He moved as if to put his arms around her in return, but his hand hovered over her without touching her, and after a moment or two, he let it fall back to his side. She tried not to let the rejection sting. Despite the kiss, he clearly wasn't interested in her. And that was fine. Really. It was. She pulled back, then sat down on the bed, watching him carefully.

"I'm really sorry about the way I acted last night," she said softly. "I was way out of line. Are you still angry with me?"

Dominic shook his head. "I'm not angry with you, Ms. Blake. I'm just trying to do my job and stay focused." He looked away for a moment, sighed, then turned back to face her. "I have to tell you, I'm also not happy that you're going to be participating in the arrest. It goes against my better judgment, like I said, but my team is convinced that this is the best chance we have of apprehending Michael." Jessica forced herself to smile. This was what she'd wanted—the chance to help her brother. That was the only reason why she was there. She couldn't let herself forget that.

"The plan is that you'll go into the restaurant and eat

brunch like a regular customer. You can't wear a vest because it would be too noticeable, but we're going to put a wire on you. Once you see him, describe him to us over the mike. If you run into trouble, you just have to say, 'it sure is hot outside.' Then we'll move in. Got it?"

She nodded.

Dominic stood. "All right. Well, Jake is making some breakfast, if you're interested. You might not get a chance to really eat anything at the restaurant, depending on the timing, so you probably should grab a bite here before we go. Jake's the resident gourmet, but there's not much here to work with, so be patient with his culinary skills."

"Sounds good. I'm actually a little hungry," she said, trying not to let the hurt come out through her voice. Focus. This was all about Michael. Nothing else. If Dominic was going to be detached, then she would have to be as well. "Give me a chance to brush my hair and clean up a little, and I'll be out in a minute."

He raised an eyebrow, and before he even opened his mouth, she knew what he was going to ask. "No running?"

She shook her head. "No. You said I could go to the restaurant with you and I believe you. You haven't lied to me yet." She met his eye. "I want to help Michael."

"Okay then. Be in the kitchen in five minutes. Jake wants to go over the wire with you and we need to leave soon so we can get everyone in place."

She watched him leave, regret eating away at her. She shouldn't have let her temper get the best of her yesterday. She had acted childishly. What she should have done was try to reason with him, not force his hand. She should have tried to talk it out. Like an adult. With patience. Now, because she'd lost her temper, she and Dominic no longer had even the comfortable camaraderie they'd found during the drive to the river house the day before. She sighed and took a deep breath. It had been much easier to face everything that was happening when she had his support and friendliness to lean on. Now she felt more alone than ever.

The next hour went by in a blur. She tried to choke down some food at the house, but, despite Jake's more than adequate biscuits and ham, she hadn't been able to eat more than a few bites. She dressed in white capri pants and a loose fitting burgundy button-down shirt that hid the wire and the stitches on her arm, and she braided her hair in a long French braid that hung loosely down her back. Dominic hadn't said a word all morning, and it had been Jake that had briefed her on what to expect and what to do in the restaurant. She had looked directly at Dominic several times, and each time, he had quickly glanced away, averting his eyes. She found herself trying to joke and be friendly with Jake to ease the tension, but it came out awkward and forced, so she finally decided silence was the best course and said nothing on the entire trip back to downtown Tallahassee.

They stopped a few blocks away from the restaurant, and the marshals let her out so she could walk the rest of the way without them being seen together. It was a beautiful morning outside, not too hot or humid yet, and she used the walk to gather her strength of purpose and determination. This was all about Michael. Nothing else.

The traffic was busy, and since it was Saturday, the sidewalks were liberally sprinkled with people going to the market on Park Street. Every Saturday, vendors offered everything from craft goods to produce throughout the small park that fronted the federal courthouse. Children walked by carrying balloons and cotton candy, and she saw several young couples just strolling around, holding hands and looking at what the various booths had to offer. A few of the children had had their faces painted, and she saw a cheetah and Spider-Man go by. She watched the kids with a sense of longing. Only a few days ago, she had also been that carefree. She wondered if she would ever feel that relaxed and happy again.

She continued on to the restaurant and went in, keeping a careful eye on the people around her. She didn't see Dominic or the other marshals, but she didn't really expect to. They were experts at fitting in with their environment, and she knew that the wire she was wearing was working and gave her instant access to their help if she needed it. It made her a little uncomfortable that they would be able to hear her conversation with Michael if she actually got to have one, but it couldn't be helped. Hopefully, she and Michael would have time for a private talk later.

She found a table that faced the doorway and took a seat, noticing the people around her as she did so. The restaurant was famous for their Saturday brunch buffet, but there were only about twenty people at the moment, so there must have been some convention or other weekend activity that had kept the large numbers of customers away.

Lord, please be with me and help me do the right thing here today. I love my brother so much, even when he makes mistakes. I don't want Michael hurt. Please help keep him safe.

"Good morning. May I get you something to drink today, ma'am?"

Jessica recognized the voice instantly and looked up into the eyes of her brother. He was dressed as a waiter, right down to the black bow tie, and his blond hair had been dyed dark brown and slicked back from his face. He also had on a fake mustache that really changed his appearance and was wearing contacts that changed his blue eyes into a dark, chocolate brown. If she'd seen him walking down the street, she probably would have walked right by him, but there was no mistaking his voice, or the intensity in his eyes once she got past the change in color.

He shook his head in a barely perceptible motion just as she was about to call him by name.

"Grapefruit juice, if you have it," she stuttered, surprised by his demeanor.

"Most people choose the buffet, but you can order off the menu instead, if you'd like." He handed her a menu and she opened it, trying to figure out why he was acting as if he didn't know her. Inside the menu was a slip of paper that didn't belong there, and she quickly read the words that he had written on the page.

Are you alone?

She looked back at her brother, wondering which

answer he wanted to hear. She finally shook her head at him and held his eyes, hoping that she could convey how much she cared about him, even though her answer was probably not the one he wanted. "The buffet does look good. I'll stick with that."

Michael looked worried and scared at the same time. In fact, if she hadn't known him so well, she might have missed the slight change in his eyes and the way his hand tightened into a fist. He carefully scanned the dining room, but didn't appear to see anyone who seemed suspicious.

"Fine choice, ma'am. I'll check to see if we have any grapefruit juice. If we don't, do you have a second choice?" He subtly slipped her a second slip of paper.

I'll meet you tomorrow at the park by the racquetball courts. You know which one. 5 p.m. Come alone.

Jessica read the note and looked back at Michael. Was he going to bolt when he left to "get her drink?" She didn't want him to go. This might be her last chance to bring him into protective custody before one of Coastal's contract killers found him and killed him. Her thoughts went to Dominic, and she also realized that considering the events of last night, if she let Michael run then this was probably the last time he'd ever let her participate in the arrest. It was now or never. She had to act and act now.

"Michael, don't go. Please. We need to talk."

He instantly frowned when she said his name, and he glared at her, his expression filled with frustration and anger.

"My name is John, ma'am. You must have me confused with someone else."

She grasped his hand, but he pulled it away and started backing away from the table, scanning the room again as he did so. She stood up and took a few steps toward him, just as Dominic and Jake seemed to appear from nowhere, pistols drawn. Both were wearing bulletproof vests and small headsets that kept them in communication with the other marshals on the scene.

"Freeze, Blake!"

Michael moved fast and grabbed Jessica, pointing a small .22 caliber gun at her head before either marshal could get off a clear shot. He held her roughly, using her as a shield as he backed away from the law enforcement officers. "I'll kill her if I have to. Now back off so I can get out of here."

TEN

A woman shrieked, and a terrified murmur rose quickly from the crowd. A couple of men stood up, but Dominic's controlled voice rose above the patrons' voices.

"Federal agents, ladies and gentlemen. Please stay calm, everyone, and stay seated." He motioned to the men who were standing, and they reluctantly took their seats again. "We're U.S. Marshals, and we'll have you out of here as safely and as quickly as possible."

Dominic's heart was in his throat as he looked at Jessica's face. She had a mixture of fear and anger written there, and her body was trembling. The terrifying thought that had to be running through her head was running through his, too. Would her own brother really shoot her?

Detachment. Distance. He couldn't think about losing her right now. He had to stay focused on Michael. They didn't want to shoot him, but they would do it if Michael forced them to. The priority in this encounter was to keep the civilians safe while taking Michael Blake into custody. No life could be more important than any other if he was to do his job correctly. With one hand, he kept his pistol pointed at Blake's head, but he held his other hand palm up, in a motion of restraint.

"Easy, Blake. You're surrounded. There are two more officers behind you. You're not going anywhere. Take a minute and think about what you're doing. We don't want anyone to get hurt."

Michael glanced behind him and saw Whitney and Chris, both wearing "U.S. Marshal"-emblazoned vests over black T-shirts with weapons drawn. He pulled Jessica even closer, and his pistol was trembling in his hand. "Stay back!" he yelled, his voice filled with desperation.

"Michael, they want to help you." Jessica pleaded softly. "I know you're scared, but please, give them a chance."

Michael didn't answer, but instead kept retreating, trying to keep all four officers in sight. He stumbled slightly but righted himself quickly, keeping Jessica firmly in front of him.

"Okay, this is what we're going to do," Dominic said in a calm voice, his hand still up in a motion of surrender. "We've got a room full of terrified people, and all they want is to get out of here in one piece. Deputies Riley and Riggs are going to direct them out of here so we can talk, okay?"

Michael blew out a breath, then nodded, again pulling Jessica even closer. "She stays with me."

"That's fine. Give us just a few minutes to get these other people out of here." Dominic gave short, efficient directions into his headset, and Jake and Chris moved quickly, motioning for the customers who had been eating in the dining room to follow them. Two ladies were crying now, but for the most part, the other people were just anxious to get out of there. The patrons followed the marshals' lead and headed for the door, although a few of them kept glancing behind them, straining for a look at the man with the gun. Once Jake had everyone outside, he pulled the door closed and locked the bolt, keeping other civilians from coming in and stepping into the line of fire.

Dominic monitored their progress on his headset, keeping his focus on Michael and Jessica. He knew Whitney had cleared out the kitchen and wait staff, so he didn't expect any interruptions as they tried to talk Michael out of firing his weapon. All four of the marshals were excellent shots, but Dominic wanted Michael brought in alive. For the case—and because Jessica would never forgive him if Michael was killed.

Michael watched as Jake took up a position by the front door, then turned to see Chris, Whitney and Dominic fanned out around him. He started backing up slowly, taking Jessica with him until he was closer to the outside wall of the restaurant. From that vantage point he could see all of the marshals, but there was also no place for him to go.

Jake returned and gave Dominic the all-clear sign, and Dominic holstered his weapon and turned back to Michael, putting both hands out this time, palms up. Michael's breathing was ragged, and Dominic could tell that he was desperate and scared. "Okay, Michael. It's just us now. We know you love your sister. We know you don't want to hurt her. What's it gonna take for you to put down that gun?"

"I just want to get out of here. I'll let her go once I get to my car and get a few miles away."

"Kelley will find you sooner or later, Michael. You've seen how he operates. They want you dead, and they won't stop until they kill you and Jessica." He paused for a moment to let those words sink in. "We'll protect you, Michael. Please put the gun down."

Dominic was moving slowly toward the two as he spoke, but he froze when Michael pushed the weapon even harder against Jessica's head. She whimpered at the pain, and the sound squeezed his heart. He suddenly knew deep down that he couldn't afford to lose Jessica, and that he would do whatever it took to keep her safe. His goal was no longer to make sure Michael survived this encounter and testified against Ross Kelley. Jessica was too vibrant, too spirited to be lost in this quest for justice. Her life made the price too high, no matter what the result. He met Jessica's eyes and willed her to stay strong. Then he focused on Michael, keeping his hands within reach of his weapon if he needed to draw and take down the target as he continued advancing.

"Stop right there," Michael demanded, his voice low and threatening.

"What are you doing, Michael?" Jessica whispered, apparently hoping he would listen to the voice of reason. "You're hurting me. Please, let go of me."

He pulled the pistol back slightly, but his expression was angry, and he didn't loosen his grip. "You brought them here," Michael snapped. "Now deal with the consequences."

"Because I don't want to see you shot down in the street," she declared emphatically. "You need the marshals to keep you safe."

"Well, thank you so much for making the decision for me," he spat, his tone heavy with sarcasm. "I'm an adult now, if you haven't noticed. I make my own decisions."

"Oh, I noticed, all right. I noticed you were indicted in Atlanta, and then I noticed when somebody destroyed my house and shot at me twice in one day. Have *you* noticed that someone is trying to kill us both? Excuse me for thinking you might need a little help."

"These people can't protect me, Jess. They've already let one witness get killed. I don't want to be next." He blew out an exasperated breath. "I can't believe you brought them here! You've jeopardized everything."

Each of the marshals had been inching forward as the siblings had been arguing, but they froze when Michael looked up and noticed their movements.

"I'll shoot her," Michael threatened as he tightened his grip on the pistol. "I want out of here."

"You're not going to shoot her," Dominic said calmly, despite the fact that his heart was beating so hard it felt like it was about to jump out of his chest. "She's your sister. Your only sister. If you kill her, you'll be alone in this world, and you don't want that."

"What I want is to get out of here," Michael said forcefully. "Back off and I'll let her go once I get a few miles away."

"No," Dominic disagreed, his body tense, ready for action. "Jessica isn't leaving, and neither are you. Take a minute and think about what you're doing. You're holding a gun to your sister's head, a sister who loves you. Everything she's done, she's done out of love for you. She brought us here because she knew you needed help and that we could give it to you. She did it because she cares about what happens to you."

Michael's eyes were filled with emotion as he considered Dominic's words. Dominic pressed on, knowing at least a small part of what he was saying was getting through. He softened his voice even more and tried to sound as nonthreatening as possible. He knew Michael was scared and frantic. He hoped with a little finesse he could still talk Michael into surrendering peacefully before anyone fired their weapons. "She's taken care of you ever since your parents died. She loves you. You don't want to hurt her."

Michael's gun hand started shaking so badly he could barely control it. He looked at Dominic and closed his eyes briefly as if gathering his strength. Dominic could have taken that moment to rush him, but instinct told him to wait and be patient. Michael was very near the breaking point, and Dominic felt that the young man before him would make the right choice if given enough time to make the decision on his own.

"Give me the gun, Michael." Dominic requested quietly, holding out his hand. "Do the right thing here."

Lord, please show him that hurting Jessica isn't the answer. Help him do the right thing.

A moment passed, then another. Michael's breathing

was labored, and his fingers were turning white where he gripped the pistol. He met Dominic's eyes and finally gave a small nod. Then he slowly released the hammer with his thumb and pointed the gun at the ceiling at the same time that he let Jessica go.

He put both of his hands up and took a step back from Jessica, making it clear that he was no longer threatening her. Dominic reached Jessica and pulled her away as Jake and Whitney grabbed Michael's arms. Jake took Michael's pistol, and the two forced him to the ground with very little effort and cuffed his hands behind his back. Then Jake handed Michael's weapon to Whitney and searched Michael, making sure he didn't have a second weapon stashed somewhere on his body.

Dominic led Jessica away from the others and held her tightly, rubbing her back with his hand while the others finished securing Michael Blake. He could feel her trembling as she let a soft sob escape against his shirt. He had been so scared for her. Relief washed over him like a summer storm, fast and frantic.

"I knew he wouldn't do it," she whispered. "But I was still scared."

He gently cupped her face in his hands and brushed away her tears with his thumbs. Her skin was still pale and her eyes large with trepidation. "It's over now. You're safe."

"It's not over," she said between tears. "It's just beginning." She glanced back at the sight of Michael on the floor, but it must have been too painful to watch him being arrested because she quickly turned back to

Dominic. "I'm still glad I came," she said softly. "Thank you for letting me come."

Dominic gave a small laugh and hugged her close again. It felt so right to have her in his arms. "I didn't have a lot of choice. You like living on the edge, don't you?"

"Not really, but it's becoming a habit." She pulled back slightly and watched as Michael was pulled to his feet and led out of the room. He kept his head down and his eyes averted. She moved to follow him, but Dominic held her back. She could only watch as he walked out of view.

It must have broken her heart to see him in handcuffs and know he was headed for jail. This was her brother. She had sacrificed so much for him and loved him fiercely, regardless of what he had done. Would Michael forgive her for her part in his arrest? Would he someday see it for what it was—an act of love? She turned back to the marshal, her pain showing in her eyes.

"Will I get a chance to talk to him later?"

Dominic nodded, glad to offer some small consolation. "Sooner than you think. We're taking him back to the safe house with us until we get a handle on this leak. We're not taking any chances." He let go of her and stepped back, looking at his watch. "We'll need to get you back to the safe house now. I'll have Whitney take you back while I clean up things here. She'll stay with you until I can get back over there."

Jessica kept looking toward the back door where they had taken Michael, and it took a few seconds for

Dominic's words to register. When they finally did, a look of surprise swept across her face. "You mean I can't go home?"

"I wish I could tell you that it's over now," Dominic said quietly. "But you were right when you said it's just beginning. Whether or not Michael decides to talk to us, once Coastal realizes that we have him in custody, they'll be even more of a threat to you."

"I can't live in that safe house forever, Marshal. I haven't had much experience with the legal process, but from what I hear, a trial could take months. I have obligations, my school job and my summer horse training jobs...." Her words trailed off as the full implication of his statement hit home. "I haven't even finished cleaning up from when they ransacked my house. This is crazy."

Dominic touched her arm lightly, but resisted the urge to pull her back into his arms. Her words were a cold reminder of how much they still had to face, how long this case could last. Now that he knew how important Jessica was to him, it was even more essential that he maintain the detachment that would let him stay focused on keeping her safe. He mentally kicked himself and took a step back. For now, she was a witness and nothing more. When the case was over he definitely wanted to pursue a relationship with her, but for now he couldn't. He had to keep his distance so he could keep his head on straight and do his job effectively.

"We'll know more after we interview your brother. After what's happened during the last few days, though, I can almost guarantee that Coastal still has you at the top of their hit list. Michael is a liability for them—an even bigger one now that he's in custody. If they can get their hands on you, they'll use you for leverage to keep Michael quiet until they can get a shot at him. Then they'll kill you both." He saw the fear cross her face, but he felt it was wise to tell her the truth up front so she could act accordingly. She needed to know what she was up against, and how vitally important it was for her to obey their rules and let them protect her. He motioned to Whitney who was just returning to the dining room.

"Whitney, can you please take Jessica back to the safe house and stay with her until we finish up here?"

"You've got it," Whitney answered, giving Jessica a warm smile. "Let's get out of here while the getting is good."

About an hour later they rolled down the safe house's driveway. Jessica was glad to get back and nearly collapsed when they arrived. Although Michael was in custody, and she wasn't thrilled about her brother being under arrest, she felt he was finally safe. A sense of relief was still settling in, and despite the circumstances, she was starting to relax a little. It was as if a giant weight had been taken from her shoulders and she was now sharing the burden with the marshals who were sworn to protect him. It actually felt good to let others help her deal with this horrific situation. Maybe it was okay to depend on others now and then and not try to do everything by herself. She had been so worried that Coastal would find Michael before the marshals and take her brother's life, but the marshals had come through for her and done everything they said they would.

Michael's behavior at the restaurant had shocked her when he had pressed the gun against her head, but despite his threats, she had never really felt Michael would hurt her. Michael talked a good game, but she knew he wouldn't shoot her, no matter how desperate he was. He had gotten scared, that was the bottom line, and he had been searching for a way out. She was glad that Dominic had done his homework and knew so much about them. The marshal had said just the right things to help Michael start thinking clearly.

Thank You, Lord, for letting the arrest happen with no one getting hurt. Please be with Michael and help him understand why I brought the marshals with me. Please help him forgive me. And most of all, please help him decide to work with the marshals to stop this drug counterfeiting once and for all.

Her thoughts turned to Dominic. He had handled the whole situation with professionalism and tact, and she was glad that she had trusted him to protect her brother from harm. She thought through the last few days and smiled to herself. Despite the handcuff incident, she really liked the marshal. She'd never been around someone who made her feel such a roller-coaster ride of emotions, though. One minute she was hot with anger, the next she was filled with fear or…what was that feeling that felt like butterflies fluttering in her chest? She refused to identify it. It didn't matter anyway. Whatever she was feeling, Dominic obviously didn't share it. He had said the kiss was a mistake, and she had seen him distance himself from her over and over again, despite the comfort he had given her after Michael's arrest. He was a master at giving mixed signals, and she doubted she could ever trust him with her heart.

She sighed, letting the emotional exhaustion sink in as she lay down on the bed. She needed a few minutes to rest and regroup. A short nap wouldn't hurt anything. Within moments, she was sleeping soundly.

ELEVEN

Dominic took a sip from his coffee cup and watched Michael Blake through the small window in the door of the large storage shed located just behind the safe house. His hands were handcuffed and chained to a heavy wooden chair, and his legs were also cuffed and chained. He pulled against the handcuffs in a defeated, useless gesture, then shifted and pulled again. He had probably never been restrained to this degree in his life, even when he was arrested in Atlanta, and it seemed as if a restless energy kept sweeping through him. If Michael hadn't threatened his sister at the restaurant, he probably wouldn't be wearing all these chains right now, but whenever Dominic remembered the frightened look on Jessica's face, he found that he had very little sympathy. Blake could have just surrendered peacefully at any time, but he had gotten scared, and had put Jessica's life in danger without even considering the repercussions of his actions.

In fact, Dominic was still wondering if Michael would have sacrificed Jessica if he hadn't been able to talk him into surrendering. He'd seen a desperation in

Michael's eyes and a frustration there that had sent great doses of apprehension down his spine. Thankfully, he had been able to talk Michael down, but it hadn't been a sure thing going into it. He said a silent grateful prayer that the arrest had taken place without anyone getting hurt.

He took another swig of coffee and watched thoughtfully as Michael's impatience got the best of him and he rattled the chains once again. Normally they would have taken him straight to intake and he would have been processed like any other prisoner, but the threat of the leak had been too great, so they had brought him to the safe house for interrogation. He'd been sitting there for quite a while chained with a limited range of motion, waiting for someone to come along and start the interrogation. At this point, Michael was probably hungry, tired and a little scared. He might not be in a hurry to talk to someone, but the desperation of his situation would definitely be weighing heavily on his shoulders by now, and every minute that passed made it worse. Dominic hoped that the longer they left him stewing in frustration, the better chance they had of working out a deal with him.

Dominic glanced over as Chris walked up and handed him a file. "Any news on our leak?"

Chris nodded. "Looks like Whitney has narrowed it down. They think it's Chuck Holiday."

Dominic leaned wearily against the building and ran his hands through his hair in a motion of resigned disappointment. The news would have been tough to hear no matter who Chris had named. Law enforcement protected its own, and loyalty was highly prized. To be a traitor to the force was quite possibly the worst thing an officer could do. Chuck Holiday, however, was an FBI agent who had been a part of the multiagency task force since the beginning, and he was Dominic's friend. Although they had never socialized together after hours, they had definitely spent plenty of time together working on the task force and combing through evidence. Chuck would have had access to all of the information about Levine's whereabouts before he was killed and also would have had enough intel to orchestrate the attempts on Jessica's and Michael's lives.

Chuck had never shared much about his personal life, but Dominic had heard rumors that the man was going through a messy divorce that was apparently ripping his entire life apart. On one hand, he felt sorry for him, but on the other, he realized that Chuck's actions had killed one man and put everyone on the task force in danger, as well as Jessica.

"Can we prove it?"

Chris shook his head. "Not yet. Everything points to him, and we're monitoring his communication and whereabouts, but we need some solid proof, some overt act, to nail him down."

Dominic nodded, absorbing the information, then looked at the folder that Chris had handed him. The top sheet was a current printout of Blake's charges in Atlanta that had been recently updated to reflect the new charges the district attorney was adding from the scene in the restaurant. Kidnapping. Attempted murder. Resisting an officer with violence. The second sheet was a brief synopsis of what they had learned about Michael from their investigation.

Dominic scanned it briefly, just to see if any new information caught his eye. He'd read the file so many times at this point that he practically had it memorized. Still, he found an interesting note buried near the end of the document about some medical supply purchases that had been made on Blake's credit card. Dominic hadn't noticed that before. Apparently Michael had bought over a hundred dollars' worth of supplies on three separate occasions, yet he didn't appear to have any legitimate reason or medical condition that warranted the purchases. It was an angle that Dominic needed to explore whenever he had a few moments alone with the Internet or a chance to assign the research to someone else. He also looked carefully for any notes about large purchases or any other clue as to what Michael had done with the money he'd gotten from the counterfeiting, but he still didn't see anything that hinted that the man was living beyond his means. What had Michael done with the cash?

Dominic turned his attention back to Michael and watched as he made his hands into fists, pounded the arms of the chair and gritted his teeth. "Come on, let's get this moving," Michael yelled to the empty room.

Dominic caught Chris's glance and raised an eyebrow. "What do you think?"

Chris smiled out of the corner of his mouth and rubbed the stubble on his chin. "Go ahead and take a stab at him. You might get him to talk. I'm thinking he's not going to play ball, though. The anger is a front, that much I can tell. But I have a feeling that there's something else going on that we're missing here."

Jake had been leaning against the wall, silently listening to their conversation, but now he pushed away and came over to the window. He glanced at Michael, then turned to Dominic and met his gaze. "Are you sure you want to do this? Chris or I could run through the interrogation if you want us to."

Dominic drained his cup, crushed it with his fist and tossed it in a nearby trash can. He understood where Jake was coming from, but he wasn't going to let his personal feelings interfere with his job any longer. He met Jake's concerned eyes with a determined look of his own. "I'm okay, Jake. I can handle this." He grinned, hoping the expression would put Jake more at ease. "I always liked playing the bad cop anyway. Today it will be easier than ever." He poured coffee from his Thermos into a fresh cup, nodded to the two men, and took the cup into the interrogation room with him and set it on the table in front of Michael within his reach. "You take it black?"

Michael ignored the coffee and watched the marshal with angry eyes. When Dominic took the chair across from him, the younger man glared at him. "Well, you've sure made me wait long enough. I've been in here for hours!"

Dominic shrugged. "Did you have an appointment to be somewhere? Sorry, you're going to miss it." The marshal's face was grim, and although he had his emotions well in control, there was still a wave of anger just below the surface that he did nothing to disguise.

"Well, I didn't plan on sitting in this room all afternoon."

"Where would you rather be? Back at Coastal counterfeiting drugs, or holding another gun to your sister's head? Hmm. That *is* a tough decision."

Michael rolled his eyes and motioned to the room. "Why'd you bring me here instead of to the jail?"

"We're trying to keep you safe. There is a leak selling information to Coastal, a leak that wants you dead."

Michael took a deep breath, absorbing the information. "So I was right. I knew it. I just knew it. I can't believe Jessica trusted you guys. Where is my sister anyway?"

"Do you really care?"

"Of course I care."

Dominic grunted. "You have a funny way of showing it."

Michael glared at the lawman. "My sister is my business, not yours. Just tell me where she is."

Dominic met the eyes of the man before him and narrowed his eyes. "Somewhere safe."

Michael raised an eyebrow. "Really? She's still in danger. You know that, don't you?"

Dominic watched him carefully. "What makes you think so?"

Michael shook his head. "You're kidding, right?"

"Well, I've got shipping manifests and other receipts with your name on them. In fact, every time our subpoena recovers another document, it points to you or Don Levine as the mastermind behind the entire counterfeiting scheme. Since Levine is dead, and you're in custody, why would Jessica be in any danger?"

Michael never blinked. He didn't volunteer any new information either. "So what's it gonna take for me to get out of here?"

Dominic shrugged. "You're not going anywhere. You racked up a list of charges here in Florida, and once you've dealt with those, you'll be given a free ride over to Georgia to face whatever you left behind up there."

It was Michael's turn to shrug. "Petty stuff. I'll be out in no time."

Dominic seethed, his voice low and threatening. "You think it's petty to put a gun to your sister's head and threaten her life?"

Michael rolled his eyes again. "You know that's not what I meant."

Dominic leaned forward. The kid's nonchalant attitude was bothering him more than he would like to admit. He had to stay focused and keep his anger under control. "Look, Blake. At this point, all the evidence points to you. That means that unless you start talking, you'll be going down on federal conspiracy and counterfeiting charges, all by yourself." He leaned back. "You and I both know Levine was murdered. If you think someone hasn't been hired to get rid of you too, you're fooling yourself. You'll never make it to trial without our help. Have you stopped to consider that?"

"I want my family protected. That's all I want."

"Yes, we know that. But you have to step up to the plate to help protect your sister."

Michael gave a short derisory laugh. "Oh yeah? And just how am I supposed to do that when I'm in here?"

Dominic looked him in the eye. "Tell us everything you know about Ross Kelley, then testify against him in court. Let us know if he has any accomplices. If you do have a disk with pertinent information in your possession, tell us where it is."

Michael didn't even hesitate. "I can't. Kelley will kill me."

Dominic shook his head. "He's already trying to do that anyway. You stand a better chance of survival if you become a federal witness. We'll protect you and your sister. You get what you want, and so do we. It's as simple as that."

"Nothing is ever that simple," Michael breathed, almost as a whisper. He pulled against the handcuffs in a motion of exasperation. "I have nothing to say to you."

"Then you're going to prison," Dominic said, his tone matter-of-fact.

Michael laughed. "For what? Those charges in Atlanta? You don't have any proof or you wouldn't even be talking to me. Levine is gone and so is your case. I don't have a record, and I'm the low guy on the totem pole anyway. I'll walk away with probation, if that."

"Actually, Blake, you're the only guy left holding the bag. We've got enough evidence to show that you were the one buying medicine from Coastal and then diluting various types of medicine under the name of Spirit wholesalers. It's your name all over the paperwork, not Kelley's."

For the first time, a flash of worry crossed Michael's face. "That's not right."

Dominic shrugged. "Like I said, that's what the paperwork says. Levine told us that Ross Kelley and Jeff Martin were the masterminds behind the counterfeiting. In fact, Levine told us that Kelley was the one who actually took care of all of the paperwork and created the phony company named Spirit wholesalers. But Levine's gone now, Kelley and Martin claim to have no knowledge of the counterfeiting, and all of the paper evidence I have points to you." He paused, letting his words sink in.

"We have inventory lists with your signature on them, showing where you received the legitimate medicine, and we have Spirit's sales records leading back to your personal computer for over a year. We also have equipment with your fingerprints on it." Dominic leaned forward. "The long and short of it is, we have everything we need to convict you, Blake, and nobody else."

TWELVE

Michael's face remained expressionless, but tiny beads of sweat started to show on his forehead, and his breathing became more labored. "None of that is true," he said suddenly, his voice vehement. "Kelley must have doctored up the paperwork. They're all forgeries. I never signed anything, and I never used my computer for any of the counterfeiting."

"That's not what the evidence says, Michael."

Michael pounded on the chair with his fist. "Well, the evidence is wrong!"

Dominic leaned in. "So help us out. Write out a statement that tells what really happened so we can prosecute the real masterminds behind this mess. Give us the disk that shows Kelley and Martin were involved. We're willing to listen to your side of things. We even believe you. That's why I'm sitting here right now, but I've got to tell you, unless you're willing to back up your story in court, everything we have points to you, and you'll be the one going down for it. Someone has to go to prison, Michael, and if we can't have them, then we'll take you." There. All of Dominic's cards were on the table. It was now up to Michael to make the next move and play out the hand.

A shuttered look came over Michael's features. "I can't. I don't even know enough about the operation to help you."

"I don't think that's true. If it were, you wouldn't have been smart enough to make a backup disk. You knew the day would come when you would need it to support your story, and that day is today."

Michael met the man's eyes but didn't respond. Clearly affected by the fact that the marshal knew so much, Michael showed his stress in his taut features. Still, he held back and refused to confirm what Dominic was saying.

Dominic pressed forward. "If you turn the disk over to us and it contains what we think it does, we'll be able to bust this case wide open."

"No!" Michael yelled forcefully. "I'm telling you that I'm not testifying. I can't."

"Can't, or won't?"

"Both!"

"Then you'll do the time in a federal prison. It's your choice."

Michael tried to look like the prospect of prison didn't bother him, but he wasn't very successful and his hands started to shake. Nevertheless, bravado colored his voice when he spoke. "So I'll just do the time. I'll probably get less than a nickel since it's my first offense. It'll be easy."

"The average sentence in these cases is twenty to life,

even for first-time offenders. And there's no such thing as easy time at a maximum security prison."

Michael glared at the lawman, clearly understanding the implicit threat.

Dominic ignored Michael's wrath and opened a folder he'd been carrying to pull out some photos. They were all eight-by-ten color photographs of a brutal murder scene, and Michael looked away, obviously sickened. "Prison is the least of your problems. These are photos of Don Levine's murder. I'm sure Don thought that he could protect himself, too." He laid out a few more photos. "See these bruises?" He held one up, even though Michael was looking in the other direction. "We think these came from a baseball bat." He picked up another photo. "Now these marks…"

"I get the idea," Michael interrupted.

"Obviously you don't if you think Kelley won't do the same to you." Dominic paused, letting his words sink in. "In fact, I think you're in even more trouble because Ross Kelley knows that you have that disk, and what's on it. He knows the same thing we do. If that disk gets found and you testify against him, it'll be the proof we need to take down Coastal's entire counterfeiting opera-tion." He paused again and leaned back in the chair. "So you see, it all boils down to this. You can either go down by yourself as the counterfeiter—provided you live long enough to get to trial—or you can tell us what really happened at Coastal and stop Ross Kelley from sending more hit men after you and Jessica. The choice is yours."

Michael swallowed. "It's not that simple."

Dominic stared at him. "Then enlighten me. Tell me what I'm missing."

Michael shook his head and looked down at the floor. "I can't."

Dominic leaned forward. "Don't be stupid, Blake. Your back is against the wall here. The only way out of this is the road I'm offering."

"I can't do it." Michael said, his voice rising. "You don't understand what you're asking me to do."

"Then you're signing your sister's death certificate. Maybe you should have pulled the trigger this morning after all. You're doing the same thing by refusing to cooperate."

Michael pulled on the chains in frustration, looking as if he wanted to get up and strike Dominic if he hadn't been cuffed to the chair. The anger made his face flush and his blue eyes flash. He grabbed for the coffee that was still sitting in front of him, but Dominic read his body language and reached the cup first, quickly moving it before Michael could toss it at him.

"I'm not playing your game, Marshal," Michael hissed. "I'll do my time, but I'm not testifying against Kelley or anybody else. You couldn't even keep Levine safe. What makes you think I'd ever trust you?"

"I agree that the leak is a problem, but we're handling it. We *will* keep you safe if you cooperate."

Michael shook his head. "I don't believe you. You'll have to find yourself a different witness. Got it?"

Dominic held his gaze. "You want to tell Jessica that, or should I?"

Michael muttered something under his breath and

looked away. He clasped his hands together, then unclasped them in a nervous gesture. Apparently Dominic's words had struck a nerve. "You'll try to protect her anyway, regardless of what I do. She can testify about how they tried to kill her. You don't even need me."

Dominic stood up and pushed away from the table, disgust making him grimace. "I doubt I'll ever be able to trace the attempted hits on Jessica back to Coastal. We all know who did it, just like we know who ordered the hit on Levine, but proving it in court is a whole other story. You're the one we need on the witness stand, not her. And let me let you in on a little secret. Jessica doesn't know a thing about the counterfeiting, and there's no way the federal government is going to spring for putting her in the witness protection program in exchange for the small amount of testimony she could offer. It's just not going to happen." He stood, still glaring at Blake with thinly-veiled contempt. "If she could, though, Jessica would switch places with you in a heartbeat, and I know that she would be tough enough to do what it took to make up for her mistakes. She'd sacrifice everything to make sure you'd be safe."

Dominic would do whatever he could to protect Jessica, but the reality of the situation was just as he had laid it out for her brother. He couldn't give her the same 24/7 protection they were giving her now if they lost Michael as a potential witness. The government didn't justify the expense of guarding someone 24/7 for an extended period of time unless the witness could offer quite a bit in testimony and that testimony was vital to a conviction. If someone were actually in the witness protection program, the government also paid for the person to have a new identity after the trial, gave them a small stipend and helped them get reestablished in a new community. None of that was cheap. Jessica just didn't know enough to justify inclusion in the program.

Michael put his head in his hands. "I've said all I'm gonna say."

"So that's your decision? You'll let Jessica die and allow Kelley to go back to distributing worthless drugs up and down the Eastern Seaboard when you're perfectly capable of stopping it?"

Michael kept his head down and was breathing heavily. "I said I'm done talking."

Dominic grabbed Michael by the collar and pulled him so close that he couldn't look away from the marshal's piercing glare. He'd had enough. Didn't Michael understand what he was risking? If he cared about Jessica at all, there was really only one option—the one Dominic was offering. Yet this guy was determined to spit into the wind. Dominic glowered fiercely at the man, and when he spoke, his voice was low and threatening.

"Listen, buddy, if you let Jessica die, there's no place you could go that I wouldn't find you. I would become your worst nightmare. You think Ross Kelley is a problem? Well, let me tell you…"

"I think I'll take over now, Deputy." Jake's voice was low and smooth as he came in and patted Dominic on the back. "Jessica is just outside, requesting a chance to speak to Mr. Blake here. Do you want to keep her company while I finish up with Mr. Blake's interview?"

Dominic got the unsaid message. Let the guy go before we lose him completely as a witness. He mentally shook himself, then loosened his grip and let Michael slide back down into his seat. "Fine. Maybe Ms. Blake would like to know how much her brother really loves her. I'll bet she'll be surprised to know that Michael wants her to just take her chances against Coastal."

"I didn't say that!" Michael said vehemently, glaring at the marshal. He pulled against his chains again, making it perfectly clear that if he was free, he would be all over Dominic. His blue eyes flashed like fire. "If I talk, someone else will die. I can't trade one life for another. I can't do it!"

Dominic raised an eyebrow. His interrogation had finally opened a door. "Whose life are we talking about?"

Michael pressed his lips together, anger and regret shooting from his eyes. When he spoke, his voice was shaking and barely under control. "I said I'm done talking."

Dominic ignored the statement. "Actually, we're just getting started. Answer the question, Michael. You're trying to protect someone. We get that. Tell us who and we'll help you."

A minute passed, then another. Michael stared at the floor and refused to look at either one of the marshals. Finally Dominic broke the silence. "What did you do with the money, Michael?"

Michael looked up, somewhat surprised. "What?"

"I said, what did you do with the money? You all must have made quite a profit by selling the phony drugs.

What did you do with your share? I don't see you driving a fancy car or living the high life in Atlanta. You must have spent the money on something. What did you do with it?"

Michael made his hands into fists and closed his eyes as if he was trying to get himself under control. A look of desperation swept over his features, and Dominic could tell that his questions had struck another nerve.

"We're going to find the money, Michael. It's just a matter of time. Where is it going to lead us?"

Michael put his head in his hands and refused to answer. It was evident from his body language that he had shut down.

Jake looked over at Dominic and caught his eye, then nodded toward the door. "Ms. Blake is still waiting to talk to Michael here. Why don't you go an' get her?"

"Sure thing, Jake. Maybe she can talk some sense into her brother."

After Dominic left, he could hear as Jake took the chair across from Michael. When he spoke, his southern drawl was unmistakable. "You know, Mr. Blake, I'd like to give you some friendly advice, cheap. Deputy Sullivan can be a real hothead sometimes, but let me tell you something. He's passionate about this job. He can either be your best friend, or your worst enemy. Before he gets back in here, you need to decide which side you want him to be on, and from where I'm sittin', you could use all the friends that you can get."

Dominic paused for a minute on the other side of the

door waiting to see if this would finally break through the resistance the witness had shown.

But it was no use. Michael didn't answer.

THIRTEEN

Dominic started to head around to the side porch where he could see Jessica standing, then paused and turned toward Chris who was leaning against the side of the building and reading through a stack of documents. "He admitted that he's protecting someone with his silence. Any ideas of who it could be?"

Chris shrugged. "I've read this file a hundred times but nobody else's name is popping up. On another front, maybe we should take another look at Spirit Wholesalers. We could have missed something. There has to be something there that links Kelley to the corporation. Hopefully he slipped up somewhere and we can catch him in the paperwork."

Dominic shook his head. "We've already had our top forensic experts go over that corporation with a fine-tooth comb. They didn't find anything."

Chris grimaced. "Well, we thought Blake was holding something back. At least now he confirmed it. If we can figure out who he's protecting and offer to help, I bet we can still get him to roll on Kelley and Martin."

"The money is the key, Chris. I'm sure of it. If we

follow the money, we'll find out who or what Blake is protecting. He's not living like a man with a fat bank account, and that money had to go somewhere." Dominic stretched out his arms trying to work the stress out of his muscles, then ran his hands through his hair. He was so frustrated it was all he could do not to go back in the interrogation room and grab Blake again to choke some sense into him. How could that kid be so nonchalant about Jessica's life being in danger? He mentally shook himself, knowing that his feelings had no place on this job and were interfering with his judgment, but he was completely unable to shed them.

He looked over to Chris as another thought came to him. "You know, I noticed some medical supplies on his credit card bill. Did anyone ever track down what he bought? The medical supplies could have been for the counterfeiting, but something tells me he bought them for a completely different reason. We need to nail that down."

Chris stood eagerly as Dominic's enthusiasm caught hold of him. "You're right. I don't think anyone has followed up on that lead yet. And why does a guy that works for a pharmacy supply distributer buy supplies from a competitor when he can get whatever he wants practically wholesale when he's on the job? I'm pretty sure I remember Coastal having some sort of special employee discount program."

Dominic snapped his fingers. "Yeah, they actually have a really good one going, something like forty percent off. So Michael must have needed something that he didn't want his boss to find out about. Why else buy it from a competitor at nearly twice the price?"

Chris smiled. "I'll get on it as soon as we finish up here. We'll need copies of those receipts to see what he bought. I'll give the medical supply company a call."

"Check his medical records from his first arrest, too," Dominic added. "I know it's only a cursory med exam, but maybe we can eliminate him having some sort of medical issue himself. I want to cover all of the bases on this."

"You got it."

Dominic turned back to see through the window that Michael was still staring at the floor. It looked like he hadn't said another word, despite Jake's gentle probing. "He's not going to help us until we find out what we're missing. Whatever it is, it's big. Something major."

Chris took a sip of his coffee and grimaced at the taste. "What about the sister? Why don't we put them together and see what comes of it? Maybe he'll say something to her that will have some value. If she can get him to open up, it would probably save us some time."

Dominic nodded. At this point, he'd gone as far as he could go with the interrogation without new information or trying a new tactic, and he doubted Jake would do much better. Jessica just might be the key to getting what they needed out of him. "Sounds good. Jake said she's anxious to talk to him. Can you guard the door while I go get her?"

"Sure thing." Chris moved by the door as Dominic

went in search of Jessica, who had left the porch while Dominic had been talking to Chris.

He entered the house, intrigued about both the medical supply issue and the money issue. What had Michael done with his share of the proceeds, and why was he buying medical supplies? He could have asked Michael about the medical supplies during the interview, but he was wary of letting Michael know they were investigating the matter. He had to find out the answer to both questions, and he had to find out fast. Once he had the answers, he could probably use them as leverage to get Michael to testify in open court, as well as to tell them where he had stashed the disk. If they lost him as a witness, they were back to square one in this case, and that was the last thing any of the team needed.

He walked into the kitchen to find Jessica standing by the refrigerator, munching on an apple as she read a couple of articles that someone had posted there with magnets shaped like various types of fish. His heart beat a little faster when he saw her, and a feeling of protectiveness invaded his senses. She had rested a little and was now wearing a sky-blue shirt that brought out the color of her eyes, but she still looked stressed and tired. Her blond hair hung loosely around her shoulders, and he had to squelch the urge to run his fingers through the silky strands.

"Jessica?"

Jessica gave him a smile, but it was only halfhearted. "Hey, Marshal." She tossed the apple core in a nearby trash can and clasped her hands in a nervous gesture. "Is Michael ready to talk?"

"Well, I just spent about an hour with him, but so far he's not cooperating with the investigation."

Jessica raised an eyebrow. "Really? Why not?"

Dominic shook his head. "Maybe you should ask him that." He met her eyes, still somewhat aggravated by the encounter. "Look, we really need his cooperation. Anything you could do to help would be appreciated." He motioned toward the door, then followed her outside.

"Jessica, do you and Michael have any friends who are battling illness and using medical supplies?"

Jessica shrugged. "I don't know anyone, but Michael and I haven't lived together for two years. He probably has a room full of friends that I've never met." She nodded at Chris as they went to the door, then at Jake who got up and gave her a chair that was facing Michael when they entered the shed. She took in Michael's prison clothing and chained hands and feet in one quick glance, and tears formed in the corner of her eyes. She tried to rush over to Michael and hug him, but Jake prevented it.

"I'm sorry, ma'am," Jake stated, true regret in his voice. "But you're not allowed to have physical contact with the prisoner. Please just sit in this chair." He motioned to the chair and gave her a smile, which somehow seemed to soften his words.

"Can we have some privacy?" Jessica asked, looking from Jake to Dominic, a plea in her eyes.

Dominic and Jake exchanged glances, but it was Jake who answered. "Yes ma'am, if you promise me that you'll stay in that chair and you won't try to touch Mr. Blake. We'll be right outside if you need us." Jessica nodded at his request, and both marshals left the shed but stayed right outside the door so they could watch the exchange through the window. Both he and Jake kept a close eye on Michael while Jessica sat down in the chair facing her brother. Even though Michael was in chains and handcuffs, they were both alert and ready to step in at the first sign of danger. After what Michael had done at the restaurant, they weren't willing to take any chances.

Jessica's heart was breaking as she watched her younger brother sitting across from her in handcuffs. She had hoped never to see him this way, and she felt a mixture of desperation for his situation as well as failure on her part. Could she have done something to prevent him from ending up in here? Could she have done a better job as a surrogate parent? Outwardly, she tried to put on a positive front, but inside she was weeping for his mistakes and the mess he had made of his life. She met his eyes that were also stormy and troubled.

"Oh, Michael, I was so worried about you. I'm so glad you're safe."

Michael looked away, clearly uncomfortable with contact. "Jessica, I'm sorry about what I did to you in the restaurant. You have to know I would never have hurt you. I was just so scared, you know? Everything was happening so fast and I didn't know what to do."

"It's all right," she answered. "I didn't think you would really shoot me."

He waited a moment, then finally looked back up and reached for her even though the handcuffs stopped him from actually touching her. "I wanted to talk to you by yourself. I thought maybe we could meet somewhere else, you know? Someplace where I could be sure Coastal wasn't tailing me or you, either. Why did you tell the police it was me?"

"Because I didn't want Coastal to get to you first. Those people destroyed my house and threatened me. They've tried to kill me twice and you at that bagel shop. It's not safe for either of us out there. You need these guys. The marshals are the only ones who can protect you."

Michael grunted. "I can't believe you trust those cops. Didn't they tell you about the leak? One of them is dirty."

"Not one of these," she answered defensively. "I know about the leak, but I also know it isn't one of these four marshals here at this house. They've risked their lives for me."

Michael's eyes darkened as they locked with his sister's. "Did Coastal really try to attack you?"

Jessica's eyes narrowed. Why was her brother being deliberately obtuse? She pulled up her sleeve and showed him the bandage. "Well, you were there at the bagel shop. What do you think?"

Michael shrugged. "I didn't know what to think. I mean, I know you got shot and everything. I guess I thought a policeman went a little crazy and fired that shot."

"That was no policeman's bullet that hit my arm, Michael. And it was also no policeman who tried to kill me at the hotel a few hours later, and certainly no policeman who ransacked my house, or who called and threatened my life. That's not the way they operate."

Something in the way she said it must have hit Michael the wrong way, and he grimaced in disgust. "You really do trust these guys, don't you? Don't you realize one of them is dirty?"

"Someone somewhere is dirty, but it's not one of these four. I do trust them. They've proven themselves over and over again, and have been nothing if not professional. I owe them a great deal."

She twisted the ring on her finger, then pulled it from her right hand and moved it to her left. Finally, she looked him directly in the eye. "Michael, they said you're mixed up in drug counterfeiting. How could you be a part of something like that?"

A look of pain crossed his face for a moment. Finally, he crumpled. "The counterfeiting is just a small part of the big picture. I was trying to help someone, and, well, the whole thing got out of hand."

Jessica sat up straighter, considering his words. "Okay. Then why not tell the marshals everything? Why not go to court and put the person who's really responsible for the counterfeiting behind bars?"

"I can't, Jess. I just can't."

"Why not?" she said testily, her voice filled with exasperation. "I don't understand. Don't you know how many people can get hurt using counterfeited medicine? You have to testify and stop them before anyone else gets hurt. It's not only the right thing to do, it's the only thing to do, especially since you can clear your name at the same time."

He met her words with stony silence, so she pressed on.

"The police are supposed to be the good guys, remember, Michael? The men you were working with are dangerous, and I've got a scar to prove it." She motioned to her bandaged arm.

Michael leaned forward and brought his voice down to a whisper. "I've got to think about more than myself here, Jess. I've done more than just the counterfeiting and if I talk about it to the cops, it would hurt some other people, maybe even cause someone's death." He swallowed and bent his head over the table toward his hands so she couldn't see the anguish in his eyes. "I'm so sorry, Jessica. I really thought I was doing the right thing, but now this thing has gotten so big, I don't know what the right thing is anymore."

Jessica wanted so badly to touch her brother and reassure him in his distress, but she knew it would bring the marshals back into the room in a rush. "Michael please," she pleaded. "Tell me what is going on."

A moment passed, then another. Finally Michael looked up, his blue eyes filled with torment. "Do you remember Sandy Parker? She was in my class at school and was kind of short with dark hair. Well anyway, I didn't bring her around the house much, but we were dating on and off for about a year. Then all of a sudden she got pregnant and moved off to Atlanta to live with her sister. When I moved out, I followed her there because…well…ah…it's my kid." He pushed on, despite seeing the surprise and distress in sister's eyes.

"I started working for Coastal as a delivery boy for

one of their pharmacies in Atlanta." He took a breath. "After the baby was born, she kept getting sick, and it took the doctors a long time to figure out what was wrong with her. Finally they discovered that she has a rare blood disease, and she needs this drug called Neupogen to help her fight infection. Without it, she'll die. Sandy works, but she doesn't make much money, and she doesn't have any insurance. She tried to get Medicaid to help, but it turns out the drug is an experimental treatment for the condition and is also really expensive, so even on Medicaid, she couldn't get the medicine the baby needs. On top of that, Sandy has missed a lot of work because she has to take the baby to the doctor so much, and she can't make ends meet, even with her sister's help."

He looked away, obviously struggling, but finally brought his eyes back to his sister. "About that same time, Coastal offered me a job at their warehouse. It was a chance to move up and make a little more money, so I took the job." He swallowed. "Once I was there, I had access to all kinds of medicine, and it was easy enough to change the quantities on the packing slips and routing software." He paused again and gritted his teeth, then plunged forward. "I've been stealing Neupogen from Coastal for over a year and giving it to Sandy under the table. I've also been using my cut from the counterfeiting to pay off the doctor bills."

Jessica couldn't believe her ears, and a wave of emotion swept over her. Michael had a child? That was a huge secret to keep. She was hurt, frantic and scared all at the same time. One minute she wanted to shake some sense into her brother, the next she wanted to hug him and tell him that somehow they could work this out together. She tried to hold her emotions in check, knowing the marshals needed little or no excuse to come charging back into the room.

"How did you get mixed up in the counterfeiting in the first place?"

Michael rolled his eyes and sank back in the chair. "Because I was incredibly stupid. There was another guy working in the warehouse named Levine. About a year ago, I saw him working with a guy named Jeff Martin. They were soaking the labels off of some of the medicine bottles and replacing them with new labels. I pretended I didn't see anything and got out of there, and then later I went back and looked at what they had been doing. They had diluted the medicine and had four times more than they had listed on the packing slip. I checked the invoices and verified what they had done, but I was afraid to tell anyone because I was guilty of stealing, so who was gonna believe me, you know? Then Levine cornered me one day with a gun. He says he knows that I know about the counterfeiting, and I could either be a part of it and make some good money, or die right then and there. Well, I wasn't a big fan of getting killed, so I started helping them with the counterfeiting." It made sense, in a horrible sort of way. What Michael had done was still wrong, but now at least she was starting to understand what had driven him to it.

"About a month ago, Levine was arrested, and he must have told them about me and the whole operation, because about a week later, I was arrested for the counterfeiting, too. Then the next thing I knew, Levine was murdered. I knew he must have been killed for talking to the feds, so I got scared and decided I had to get out of there as soon as I got bonded out." He shook his head. "I'd been saving scanned copies of all of the doctored paperwork on a disk, since I knew that it was illegal. I figured Martin wouldn't hurt me as long as he knew I had the disk and that the feds could use it as evidence. You know—I won't give the disk to the cops, you don't kill me."

"Michael, you have to give the disk to the marshals. It's the only way out of this."

He gave her an incredulous look. "Have you been listening to me at all? I did a lot more than the counterfeiting. They're not going to want my testimony if they find out about the stealing, and now that the paperwork has been doctored to make me look like the guilty one, they're not even going to believe what they see on the disk."

"Of course they will. They have experts who can verify the paperwork. And they only care about taking down Coastal's counterfeiting scheme. I'm sure they'll let you plea bargain the other stuff away. All you have to do is testify about what you know and give them the disk for evidence."

Michael gave a short derisive laugh. "So now you're a lawyer?"

Jessica leaned forward, her blue eyes flashing. "No, I'm a realist. I've been talking to these marshals for several days. There's a federal case pending against Coastal that's worth a lot more to them than some petty theft charges."

"You make it sound so simple, but it's really not, and I'm not going to the cops regardless."

"Regardless of what? Do they actually have to *succeed* at killing you or me before you take Coastal's threats seriously? Somebody at that company wants us both dead. Are you missing that part of the picture here?"

"What do you think they'd do if they knew I had a daughter?" Michael whispered looking at the door to make sure the marshals didn't come back in. He shook his head and narrowed his eyes. "Once Coastal makes the connection, they'll go after her just like they're going after you. You actually have a chance of escaping them, but my daughter doesn't have any chance at all."

Jessica didn't have an answer for that one. She let out a breath and looked away. Michael was right. There was no winning answer in that equation. "Well maybe…"

"Maybe? Do you hear yourself? Maybe isn't good enough. What if I tell the marshals everything and they make promises they can't keep? What happens then? I know you trust them, but I sure don't. What happens if that leak of theirs lets the news of my daughter slip?" He stared hard, his expression pleading. "Jessica, you're my sister and I love you. The last thing I ever wanted to do was put you in danger. But I have to tell you, I honestly don't know what the right answer is here. How can I choose between your life and my daughter's? I don't want her hurt because of my stupid mistakes. How can anyone say one life is more valuable than another?" He broke eye contact and put his head down on the table. When he spoke again, his words were barely audible. "I'm so scared. I tried to keep my relationship with Sandy a secret, but what if someone at Coastal found out? Every day I wake up and wonder if she and my daughter are even still alive. For all I know, Ross Kelley has already had her killed in some mysterious 'accident.'" He closed his eyes and his whole body seemed to be trembling. "Oh, Jess. I'm so sorry. I just keep making one mistake after another. I never meant to hurt you, and I sure didn't want you dragged into this. I can't seem to even think straight anymore."

Jessica was silent for a long while, mulling over everything that Michael had said. There was nothing she could do about the past, but there had to be a way to work out the future so that everyone was safe. She finally spoke, patience and love filling her voice. "What's your daughter's name?"

Michael looked up and gave a soft smile for the first time. "Julia. She's beautiful, Jess. Sandy won't let me see her much, but she's got this gorgeous smile, you know? I can't wait for you to meet her."

Jessica was silent again, then smiled back at him. The idea of meeting her niece once this was all over was very appealing to her. "Michael, everything is going to be okay. I forgive you for what happened at the restaurant, and we'll work through the rest of this together. At some point, though, you're going to have to learn to trust someone other than yourself. You don't have to do this alone. I can't speak for all law enforcement everywhere, but Deputy Sullivan and these other marshals here at the house have done everything that they said they would and then some. I trust them. I really do." She took a deep breath. "Michael, have you prayed about this?"

Michael looked up, surprised. "Have you?"

"Actually, I have. I decided I needed God back in my life right after this whole thing started. I had kind of fallen away from my relationship with the Lord, but now I'm working on making it right again. He'll give you the strength you need to do the right thing too, Michael. I just know it. Please pray about this and ask Him for help."

Michael looked away again and didn't answer for several moments, but finally he met her eyes, and there were tears in his own. "Will you pray with me?"

Jessica nodded, love filling her heart. "Absolutely." She leaned forward and closed her eyes. *"Dear God, please be with my brother and give him peace about this entire situation. We don't know the right answers, God, but You do. Please help Michael make wise decisions and help him understand that he is not alone, and that You will always be with him. Help us both to trust You, and strengthen us to do Your will. And most importantly, God, please help us to stay alive and get us through this ordeal, and help us figure out a way to help Michael's baby girl get the medicine she needs. Amen."*

FOURTEEN

Dominic glanced through the window. "He hasn't moved an inch since he asked to be alone to think, and that was over half an hour ago," he said to Jessica, who had returned from getting a soda to join him by the shed's door. "You did a great job of talking to him."

She looked up at Dominic and smiled, feeling hopeful and stressed at the same time. "You could hear all that?"

"Bits and pieces. The door is not as soundproof as Michael seems to think. I didn't know about Julia. It answers a lot of questions."

"I have to admit I was shocked to hear that I'm an aunt. That's not the kind of news I was expecting, you know?" She reached over and squeezed his hand, then quickly released it when he tensed and took a step back. She pressed on, trying to pretend that the distance he had put between them didn't affect her, even though the hurt swept through her from head to toe. Had she really been thinking of trusting this man with her heart? He couldn't have made it more clear that he wanted to keep her at a distance. She forced her thoughts back to

Michael and the problem at hand. There would be plenty of time for recrimination later.

"I feel so sorry for that little girl with her medical issues. There's got to be something that can be done to make sure she gets the medicine she needs." She leaned against the building, her hands in her pockets so she wouldn't be tempted to touch him again.

"I can't believe he's a father. Especially since just a few years ago he was a kid himself. Michael was really different when he was younger, if you can believe it. He was always eager to please, and went out of his way to help me out around the farm. I remember once when he was about thirteen, I got thrown off a horse and hurt my ankle. He had seen the accident through the window and came barreling out to the barn as fast as his legs could carry him. Michael never liked the horses the way I do. In fact, he was always a little afraid of them, but he ran into the corral just the same, right past the horse I was training that was still acting a little wild and crazy. He helped me to the house and got me an ice pack, and the rest of the week, he was always at my elbow, eagerly trying to help me out with whatever I needed." She closed her eyes, remembering. He had been so young then and so full of promise. It broke her heart to see the man he had become and the life he was facing. A sob tore from her lips, and she could do nothing to hide it. Her determination to maintain distance from Dominic crumbled, and she threw herself into his arms, crying the tears that had been threatening ever since she had seen her brother arrested at the restaurant.

The last few days had been an emotional roller coaster

for her, and for the first time since this whole thing had started, she let herself express all of the feelings that had been bubbling up inside of her. The marshal was warm and smelled of coffee and mint, and his touch was immensely comforting. She knew he was offering nothing more than friendship, especially since he had stiffened when she touched him, but she was grateful for the shoulder to lean on nonetheless. Friendship was better than nothing.

"It's all right. Everything's all right," he soothed.

"No, it's not," she sobbed. "He's made some big mistakes, Dominic, and so have I. I should have been there for him. Why didn't I see what was happening? Why didn't he tell me?" She paused, the tears flowing freely down her face. When she spoke again, her voice was barely above a whisper. "This is not how I envisioned his life would turn out, you know? I had really big dreams for him." She pulled back and looked into the marshal's eyes, her own wide and troubled. She sniffed and took a deep breath, trying to control her tears. It seemed impossible. "My heart hurts. I mean really hurts. It feels like someone is squeezing it and will never let go."

Dominic pulled her close again, letting her cry. He simply held her until she was spent, and her tears slowed. After a few moments, he went in search of tissue and returned with a box, letting her blow her nose and catch her breath. She leaned against him, and he put his arm around her, offering her his comfort and friendship.

"Jessica, Michael is young and his life is just beginning," he said. "He made some bad choices, but they were his choices, not yours. You can't live his life for him. He's an adult now and has to live with the consequences of his actions. I agree that he's made some big mistakes, but he still has plenty of time to turn things around and do the right thing, both for himself and for his daughter. Testifying against Coastal will go a long way toward making things right."

She took a deep breath and wiped her nose. "Thanks for saying that."

Dominic gently touched her chin and raised her head so that their eyes met. "I meant it."

She gave Dominic a tremulous smile. "I know you did. Thanks for listening to me, Marshal, and letting me cry on your shoulder. I know it can't be easy for you when I have these emotional outbursts right in front of you." She paused, horrified at the realization of what she'd done. "I didn't mean to throw myself at you like that." She hugged herself, suddenly feeling awkward and out of place. The pink tint of embarrassment colored her cheeks, and she couldn't get out of there fast enough. She took a step back, then turned, averting her eyes. "I think I'll go back inside. Will you call me if Michael wants to talk to me again?"

"Absolutely."

Jessica quickly fled into the house, but found that the tiny space wasn't much of an escape from all of the thoughts that were swimming around in her head. She paced back and forth in the little living room, but after a minute or two, the walls seemed to be closing in on her. What she really wanted was to go for a long walk along the river to sort everything out, but of course, that wasn't a possibility any time in the near future.

Ugh! How could she have just thrown herself in Dominic's arms when the man obviously didn't want to pursue a relationship with her? She needed to back away, just as Dominic had. If she didn't, she'd end up with more than just a broken heart. She'd end up humiliating herself. She sighed, disgusted with herself and her lack of control.

She forced her thoughts away from Dominic and tried to focus on Michael's daughter, instead. Her heart was breaking every time she thought about Julia and the future the little girl faced without the Neupogen she needed to survive. Not to mention the danger she faced from a different source—Coastal's hit men. That turned her thoughts to Coastal and the counterfeiting. In addition to the lives they endangered with diluted drugs, they had already killed one man, and had made two attempts on her life so far. The only way to end the threat that they represented to so very many people was for the marshals to stop them once and for all. And the only way for *that* to happen was for Michael to see the truth—that they couldn't make things right without his help.

She thought about Michael and smiled ruefully to herself. Faults and all, he was her brother and only living relative. She loved him unconditionally and could well understand how he had gotten into the counterfeiting, and why he was so scared to testify now. He should have gone to the police when he had first found out about the illegal activity, but with little Julia's life hanging in the balance, she could see why he had made the choices he'd made. Of course it was also wrong to steal, even if it had been for Julia's sake, but Jessica sympathized with the torment Michael and Julia's mother were going through right now as they worried about the girl's fragile medical condition.

Since Michael had been arrested, their supply of Neupogen was cut off, and she doubted Medicaid had had a change of heart and suddenly decided to start covering the cost of the expensive drug. There had to be a way to continue helping the child without breaking the law, though. There just had to be.

She wrapped her arms around herself and groaned in frustration. She had to do something. She knew Whitney was in the house somewhere, so she went in search of her and found her in the kitchen, grimacing over a pot of coffee.

"Hey, Whitney."

Whitney turned. "Hey." She continued to pour the coffee down the drain, then washed and rinsed out the pot and put it on the dish rack to dry.

"Do you think I could use your laptop to do a little online research?"

Whitney opened a cabinet, searching the contents. "Why?"

Jessica pursed her lips. "Well, I was hoping to find out a little more about drug counterfeiting. I don't know much about it and thought some research would help." Whitney's face registered wariness, so Jessica pushed forward. "Look, I have to do something. I'm going a little crazy in here."

Whitney seemed to consider her words, then finally shrugged. "I guess it's okay with me, but there are a few rules. You can't check any of your e-mail, or go to any of the sites where you have log-in information stored on the site. If you log on under one of your user names and passwords, Coastal can pick up your log-in and trace it to your location with a simple software program."

"No problem," Jessica said quickly, agreeing to the terms. "The last thing I want right now is to tip off Coastal as to where to find me."

Whitney set up the laptop in the living room and signed her on. Jessica thanked her as the marshal headed back to the kitchen. Then Jessica returned to the keyboard and, with a few quick strokes, found her favorite search engine and typed in "drug counterfeiting." The whole concept was still foreign to her and seemed like something that existed in a third world country twenty years ago rather than in the modern-day United States. She wanted to find out more about the crime to see the big picture and fully understand the enormity of what Michael had gotten himself into.

Her search instantly rewarded her with several articles, and she read two or three before sinking back in the chair. What she discovered made her heart sick. According to the Internet, drug counterfeiting, when done by experts, was capable of doing incredible damage while being almost impossible to track.

And according to the articles, those who were successful at counterfeiting were able to make millions of dollars with very little risk of punishment. No wonder the marshals were so determined to get Michael's testimony—and no wonder Ross Kelley was so determined to silence Michael at any cost.

She rubbed her eyes. She was still emotionally exhausted from everything that had happened in the last few days. She disconnected from the Internet and leaned back, closing her eyes against all of the thoughts that were pelting her from so many different directions. Within a few moments, she was napping.

There was something touching her arm. It was a soft sensation at first, then seemed somewhat rougher, pressing against her skin. She moved to brush it away, then felt another touch on her other arm which frightened her. She starting twisting and fighting, trying to free herself from whatever was disturbing her and restraining her arms. The more she fought, though, the more she felt herself become restricted and pinned to the couch.

"Let me go!" she pleaded, her voice breathless with fear.

"Whoa, Jessica. It's just me. Take it easy."

Dominic's voice broke through her sleepy haze, and she quickly calmed down and quit fighting him. Finally awake, she willed away the images from her dream. She had been locked in a small dark room and tied to a chair. The only illumination had been a bare bulb hanging from a wire above her, but it was bright enough for her to know that she was trapped and couldn't escape. Then an evil-looking man had been standing over her, threatening her with a ferocious sneer and a very large knife. He wanted to know where the disk was, and he wanted to know now.

Jessica shook her head and closed her eyes, again trying to clear her mind of the frightening images. It took her a full minute to figure out where she was and what she was doing there. She looked around the room, and it all came rushing back. Dominic. Michael. The river house. She was lying on the sofa in the living room where she had apparently fallen asleep. The light was on in the kitchen, and it let in just enough light to see the outline of Dominic's features. Thankfully, he looked nothing like the man in her nightmare. In fact, he looked just the opposite. He had changed since the arrest at the restaurant and was now wearing a pair of khakis and a navy shirt that had U.S. Marshal embroidered on the pocket, and his casual clothes gave him a laid-back and approachable appearance. His slate-gray eyes seemed tired but caring, and his five o'clock shadow made him even more attractive in a roguish sort of way.

"Sorry," she whispered softly. "I was having a pretty bad nightmare. I forgot where I was for a minute there."

"I didn't want to wake you," Dominic whispered. "Michael wants to talk, though, and I knew you would want to be in on it." He gave her a wry look. "Remind me never to wake you up again. A guy could lose a limb taking you on."

Jessica yawned and stretched, reaching for the ceiling. "For some reason, I just can't feel sorry for you. After all, you're the big strong marshal with the handcuffs." She gave him a tired smile. "How long was I asleep?"

"Just for half an hour or so. Find anything interesting on the Internet?"

"More than I wanted to know, actually. I learned a lot about drug counterfeiting. It's really a horrible crime, with only a few people regulating it. No wonder it was so enticing to the people at Coastal. I'll probably think twice now every time I get a prescription filled."

Dominic nodded. "You're absolutely right. It's more widespread than most people think, and it can hurt thousands. That's why we've been working so hard to shut them down." He stood and offered her a hand to help her get up. "Ready to go?"

It was only a courteous gesture, but she gladly accepted his hand and followed Dominic outside, hopeful that Michael had decided to cooperate.

Inside the shed, Michael was still chained in pretty much the same position where she had left him, but now there were a few more chairs in the room, and Whitney stood guard at the door. Jake and Chris were sitting a few yards away on the edge of the work table, and they both smiled and nodded when she and Dominic walked in. She nodded back and took a seat and looked closely at her brother. The stress was evident around his eyes, which were red-rimmed and heavily lined. He looked as if he'd aged ten years in just the last few hours.

"Michael, how are you doing?"

Her brother shrugged in a defeated gesture and blew out a breath. "I've been thinking, thinking a lot, actually. You were right, Jess. I'm going to cooperate and help the marshals get the disk."

"That's great news, Michael!" She reached out to hug him, but Dominic touched her arm and silently stopped her, so she sat back again.

"I hid the disk with some of the Neupogen. I wanted

to get that medicine to Sandy, but I guess that can't happen now, right?"

"The medicine is stolen property," Jake answered. "But we want to find a way to help your daughter if we can."

Michael pressed on. He seemed to understand that there were certain realities here that couldn't be changed. "First of all, I want you to guarantee Sandy and Julia's safety. Can you do that?"

Jake nodded. "If you give us what we want, we'll make sure they are protected."

Michael raised an eyebrow. "Guaranteed?"

Jake glanced at Dominic, then back to Michael. "I'll give you an honest answer. There are no guarantees in life, but I give you my word that we will do our best to protect them. Will that suffice?"

Michael seemed to consider his words, then pressed on. "That'll have to do." He paused and gritted his teeth, clearly struggling with his decision to talk, but also knowing he didn't have a lot of options. "Do you know that old airfield north of Tallahassee on Highway 27? There's a broken-down plane in one of those pole barns right by the landing strip, and a big hangar behind it at the end of the runway with a couple of more broken-down planes inside. You can get in the hangar 'cause the guy that owns it never locks it up. Way in the back left corner, there's an office that still has electricity. A friend of mine used to let me stay there sometimes. In the office is a small refrigerator, and that's where I hid the Neupogen for my daughter, along with the disk.

There's a small brown bag in the back, and the medicine and the disk are in there together. You got it?"

Jake nodded. "Yeah, I know where you're talking about."

Michael looked pointedly at Jake. "You say that Martin and Kelley have framed me for the counterfeiting and left a trail of evidence leading right to me. Well, that disk has scans of every slip of paperwork that I was aware of that had to do with the counterfeiting. It'll tell you the truth about who was in charge and how they had the counterfeiting set up."

"Are there any other copies of that disk floating around?" Chris asked.

Michael shook his head. "I only have the one."

Jake rubbed his chin thoughtfully. "You know, we could just drive over and retrieve the disk, but I'm thinking there might be a better way to go about it. We know Martin is in town, and we could get a surefire conviction if we caught him trying to destroy the disk. After all, the disk is evidence of a crime. Trying to destroy it would be a felony. We also need to draw out our leak and get evidence against him. Why don't we set a trap and catch both of them in one fell swoop?"

"That makes sense. What did you have in mind?" Chris asked, his voice filled with interest.

"Well, we could call Chuck Holiday and let him know that Jessica has escaped our custody, and that we think that Michael has sent her to retrieve the evidence. Then we let her log into her Internet account at a coffee house or somewhere. Since we know that Chuck is monitoring it, we can put surveillance in place and gather evidence against him when he notifies Martin to let him know Jessica's plans. When she goes to the airport to get the disk, we arrest Martin who will undoubtedly show up to get the disk for himself."

"No," Dominic said forcefully. "Back the truck up and wait a minute. Jessica has already been the bait twice. It's not safe."

Jake met Dominic's glare, his own eyes filled with determination. "Have you got a better plan?"

Dominic stood, his stance intimidating. "I'm sure I could come up with one, given enough time."

Chris shook his head. "Time is not on our side. We can't keep Jessica away from the task force forever. This situation calls for a strong offense. We need to move on silencing this leak and catching Martin while he's here in town. If we can get Martin now, proving the rest of the counterfeiting should be a slam dunk once we have that disk in our possession."

"Do you hear what you're saying?" Dominic said, sounding exasperated. "Martin will definitely try to kill Jessica at the airport."

"And we'll be there to stop him," Jake finished for him. "Look, the bottom line is that the decision is ultimately up to Jessica." He turned to her. "What do you say, Jessica? Are you up for baiting our trap?"

Jessica looked at Dominic and could actually feel his disapproval radiating toward her. His steel gray eyes were implacable. He wanted her to say no, there was no doubt about it in his expression or body language.

She looked over to Michael, who couldn't seem to make up his mind one way or the other. Indecision was written clearly across his features just as plainly as frustration was written across Dominic's.

And as for Jessica? She wanted this over with, and she was being handed a golden opportunity to finish it, once and for all. "I admit that being a schoolteacher didn't train me for this type of thing, but I want to stop Coastal before they hurt anybody else. Sign me up."

"Good girl," Jake said, smiling as he leaned over and patted her shoulder. "We'll be right there, backing you up. This should wrap everything up. We'll catch Chuck Holiday in the act and arrest Martin all in one fell swoop. Once we get Martin in custody and get the disk, the D.A. will be ready to take the real criminals to court and all of the evidence will be pointing at the right people."

Dominic caught Jessica's eye, and she could see the anger and aggravation there penetrating through her. He left the shed and stalked purposefully outside, letting the door slam shut behind him.

She followed him, not far behind. He was taking such long strides that she had to run to catch up to him, but she matched his pace.

"Look, I know you're not happy about this…."

Dominic rounded on her. "Not happy about this? When are you going to learn? Jessica, those men want you dead! Have you forgotten that little detail?"

"Of course I haven't," she responded forcefully. "But this is the right thing to do."

"It's not safe," he said just as forcefully, accenting each syllable. "If you keep letting Coastal take shots at

you, eventually they just might succeed. And what if I can't stop them? What if I can't keep you safe and one of Coastal's hit men gets you in his sights?"

Jessica took a step back as he advanced. "Just because you're frustrated doesn't mean…"

"Frustrated?" he asked incredulously, taking another step toward her. "You think I'm just frustrated? I've got a newsflash for you, Jessica. I'm way past frustrated. I'm angry and terrified at the same time!"

"But you'll be there to protect me, you and your whole team."

"And we're good," Dominic said vehemently, "but we're not invincible. Even at our best, we're only human, and despite training and instinct, people make mistakes. We'll do our absolute best and prepare for every possibility, but this could still turn out badly, and if it does, the one who will pay the price will be you. What makes it even worse is that there's a leak out there—a leak in law enforcement, of all places. That alone makes this twice as risky." He turned to leave her again, but she grabbed his arm and stopped him.

"Dominic, right from the start, you've asked me to trust you. It was hard for me at first, but I've learned that you're a man of your word, and I also know that you and your team are as professional as they come. Now it's your turn to show that you trust me. I know there is a risk, but I accept that. I can do this, and what's more, I *want* to do this."

Dominic put his hands on his hips, his lips drawn into a thin tight line. "I don't like it. I don't want you to get hurt. These guys from Coastal don't play by the rules.

They will do whatever they have to do to win. It's just plain too dangerous."

"I know it's dangerous, and I appreciate your feelings, I really do, but this is something *I* can do to stop the counterfeiting. It's my chance to fight back. Please trust me and give me this chance to do my part."

Dominic stared into her eyes. "What if you get shot again? What if you get killed?"

"Then I'll give my life trying to do the right thing." She saw his jaw tighten, and she reached up and touched his cheek lightly. "Please, Dominic. Try to understand why I need to do this."

He covered her hand with his own and gave it a gentle squeeze. This time when he spoke, he softened his tone. "What if I can't protect you out there? I don't think I could live with myself if you got hurt on my watch."

Jessica gave him her most determined look. "I'm going into this with eyes wide open—really I am. I understand the risks and I accept them."

He swallowed, clearly exasperated. "Isn't there any way I can talk you out of this?"

She shook her head. "Sorry."

He released her hand and took a step back, then another. His expression was grim. "Okay, Jessica. If you're sure that this is what you want, I guess I can't stop you." He turned and left her standing by the shed, a tremendous sense of loss consuming her.

FIFTEEN

"Chuck? It's Dominic."

Chuck Holiday glanced surreptitiously around the room and lowered his voice into the phone. There were a few other agents in the room, but no one seemed to be paying any attention to him or his call. His shoulders sagged in relief. "Dominic, what's going on? I haven't heard from you since yesterday afternoon. Are you all right?"

"Yeah. We got Michael, Chuck, and he's willing to talk."

Chuck sat down heavily, yet still tried to instill his voice with enthusiasm. "That's great news. Can you tell me where you are? I'd like to come out and sit in on the interviews." He picked up a pen and prepared to write down whatever he could get from the marshal's call.

"Sure, that's not a problem, but we do have another issue we need to deal with first. Michael admitted that he made a disk filled with scans of Coastal paperwork dealing with the counterfeiting, but he wouldn't tell us where he stashed it. Now the sister has escaped our custody. We think Michael told her about the disk and she's planning on retrieving it herself. Our first priority has to be getting her back into protective custody as soon as possible before Coastal makes another attempt on her life. We also need that disk. It's probably the evidence we need to blow this case wide open. Do you think you can help us monitor the intel coming into the office there? I'm with Jake and we're running down a few leads. We're trying to catch up with her before she gets killed."

"What about Michael?"

"Oh, he's safe, don't worry. We'll be bringing him in as soon as we can track down the sister."

Chuck rubbed his face that was suddenly wet with sweat. "Sounds good, Dominic. Keep in touch, huh? I'll start checking e-mail and phones in case she happens to tip us off to her location or her plans. If I find her trail, you'll be the first to know."

"Thanks, Chuck. We'll sit down and coordinate everything once we have the disk and get the girl back in custody."

Chuck disconnected and leaned back wearily in his chair. Now that the marshals had Michael and were close to getting that disk, the whole operation was in jeopardy yet again. He closed his eyes for a moment but couldn't stop the feeling of trepidation that was pulsing down his spine. It seemed as if he was trying to keep a dozen balls flying up in the air, and it was just a matter of time before one or all of them came crashing down around him.

Which disaster would strike first? Would he get caught feeding information to Coastal? Would his wife's divorce attorney call him with yet another unreasonable demand? His wife had already taken everything he had of value, but he had learned not to underestimate her greed. In fact, if it weren't for her, he never would have started down this path in the first place. He knew what he was doing was wrong, yet at this point, he was desperate and already in so deep that he didn't see any way out of it. Prison was a certainty if anyone ever discovered what he was doing, so now he stayed involved not just for the money, but also to ensure his tracks stayed covered.

He pulled a package of antacid tablets out of his pocket and quickly stuffed a few in his mouth, then grimaced at the chalky taste. He couldn't stop now. It was far too late for second thoughts or recrimination. He sighed and turned back to his computer. His fingers flew over the keyboard as he began searching for Jessica Blake. She was a novice, a country schoolteacher, and it would only be a matter of time before she surfaced. When she did, he would eliminate the problem, once and for all.

"Did it work?" Dominic asked Jake, his face tense.

Jake grinned as he looked up from his laptop screen. They'd worked feverishly to set up the hotel room as a communication center for their operation, and now the trap had finally been sprung. "It looks like Chuck called Martin from an old cell phone right after he hung up with you. We got a recording of his call that should do nicely as evidence in court. He promised Martin he'd call if Jessica left any traces of her whereabouts. Looks like you should definitely expect company out at the airfield," he added, turning to Jessica, "but don't worry. You won't be there alone."

Jessica nodded. Jake's steady, determined voice helped her regain her strength of purpose, and she smiled appreciatively. She was confident that he knew his way around the latest technology, and that he had spent quite a bit of time checking and rechecking everything so that their trap was properly set. The marshals had been professional since the beginning, and their confidence helped ease the anxiety she was feeling.

Jake nodded toward Dominic who approached her with a wire similar to what she had worn at the restaurant when they had arrested Michael. "Let's get you wired for sound."

She nodded and took off her blue button-down shirt, leaving on the white tank top underneath. The other marshals turned away and started a technical conversation about computers as Dominic laid out the supplies he needed. She noticed Dominic was watching her carefully as he began attaching the wire. "Are you ready for this?"

Jessica smiled at him, trying to reassure both Dominic and herself. "You bet. Let's do it."

Dominic touched her chin gently but forced her to meet his eyes. "Are you sure? I don't want you hurt, Jessica, and you don't have to do this. You can still change your mind. We can come up with another plan." When she didn't answer right away, he pushed on. "Nobody would think any less of you if you decided you didn't want to go through with it."

The concern she saw in those gray depths was almost her undoing, but she stiffened her spine. "I'm sure, Dominic. Martin won't show unless I do. You know that as well as I do." She could tell that Dominic didn't like her answer, but he grimaced and continued with the wire. Apparently, he understood that arguing was futile. When he was finished, he tested it a couple of times to get the correct audio level, then met her eyes again.

"Now if you get into trouble, you just say 'Coastal's going down,' then we'll move in immediately. Got it?"

"Got it." She paused. "Do you think Martin will show up by himself, or bring a couple of friends?"

"We're just expecting Martin. Once you log in to your e-mail at the Internet café, I'd expect him to track you there himself to follow you to the airport. From what we know about him, he seems to be a loner. Once we're done at the airport, Jake will secure all of the electronic evidence he's getting against Chuck and we'll take him into custody. Jake put a special program on Chuck's computer that's tracking every keystroke, so when everything is said and done, we'll have plenty of proof that Chuck is our leak and that Martin and Kelley are the true masterminds behind the scheme, not Michael."

Jessica nodded. "What do you want me to try to get Martin to say?"

"Anything you can about the counterfeiting, what he thinks is on the disk and what he plans to do with the disk once he has it in his possession."

She waited for him to finish with the wire, then

slowly buttoned her shirt again to conceal it. Her mind was whirling with each button that she fastened. She wanted to do this for a myriad of reasons. Of course, it was mostly because she wanted to help her brother. Once the marshals had the disk, it would prove once and for all that Michael hadn't been the driving force behind the counterfeiting. There was a bigger picture here, however. The counterfeiting had to be stopped before even more people got hurt by taking the phony medications.

She wondered fleetingly if the CEO and Martin had even considered the impact their actions would have on the rest of the Coastal workers. Coastal was a huge corporation and was much more than just a small group of greedy conspirators. Many honest people depended upon Coastal for their living, and the entire corporation would already suffer—if not close its doors completely—once the counterfeiting was revealed and proven in a court of law. The press would eat them alive as soon as the convictions went through, that was a given. She wished there was something she could do to help all of those employees who would probably lose their jobs, but it just didn't seem to be within her power. At least she could keep innocent victims from buying adulterated medications. That would have to be enough.

Dominic stared intensely. "Please don't take any crazy chances out there, okay? If you start feeling like you're in danger, don't hesitate. Call us in. Got it?"

"Got it." She touched his cheek tenderly, pleased when he didn't pull away. "Don't worry so much. Everything will work out fine." She wished she could erase the anxiousness in his expression, but she knew the only way to do that was to decide not to go after the disk, and that simply wasn't an option.

She looked deep into his stormy gray eyes and hoped the love she was feeling for him wasn't too transparent. He was a very special man, with a big heart that was evident in everything he did, whether it was protecting her from flying bullets or handcuffing her to a chair to keep her safe. She knew he didn't share her feelings and had constantly tried to put distance between them, but she couldn't help the love that was simply brimming over in her heart. She grimaced, not wanting to humiliate herself. One way or another, she was going to have to bury these feelings. She turned quickly before she said or did something she would later regret and grabbed the keys to the little sedan she would be driving first to the Internet café and then to the airfield. "Are we ready?"

Dominic took a moment to answer, and when she glanced at him again, there was a strange look on his face that he was quick to hide. "Yes, we're ready. We've confirmed that Chris is already in place at the airstrip, and Whitney is staying with Michael. Wait thirty minutes to give Jake and me time to get there and get everything set up and to make sure Martin's on your tail, then head over to the airport yourself. The wire is already on, so if you need help with anything, go ahead and talk normally, and then we'll call you on this cell phone." He handed her a phone, and she felt a jolt of electricity as their fingers touched. He pulled back quickly. "Any questions?"

Jessica shook her head. "No, I'm set. I'll see you

soon." It seemed like a silly thing to say, but she was at a loss as the rejection swam within her once again. She tamped it down ruthlessly and tried to focus on the job at hand. This was about clearing Michael and stopping Coastal; nothing more, and nothing less.

The two men grabbed their equipment and headed out to the car. She watched through the window as they drove away, then paced and kept checking her watch until it was time for her to leave. She was nervous, yet somehow also strangely exhilarated by everything that was taking place. Training to become a schoolteacher had never prepared her for something like this, but it sure gave her a new perspective on life and a much greater appreciation for those who had chosen a career in law enforcement.

Once Jessica arrived at the café, she ordered her coffee and stirred it anxiously as she waited for the laptop she was using to log in. She knew in her heart that no one from Coastal was tracking her yet, but this was the first step, and once she started down this road, there was no turning back. She was sure she was doing the right thing, but that didn't mean that she could easily quell the nervousness that was twisting in her stomach. She said a silent prayer for strength and took a sip of her coffee, hoping that the fear that she was feeling on the inside wasn't evident on the outside.

The computer blinked to life as she was connected, and she navigated to her e-mail Web site and typed her log-in name and password. It would only take Chuck Holiday a few minutes to discover her location, but she needed to give him time to contact Martin. She checked a few of her other e-mail messages as she had been instructed to do, then finally disconnected, packed up the laptop and exited the café.

She drove toward northern Tallahassee on Monroe Street, passing Lake Ella and Lake Jackson on the way. It only took her a few more minutes to reach her destination. She surveyed the small airport as she pulled into the parking lot. There were two small buildings and a mobile home a good distance from the hangar, but she didn't see any cars and the grass was overgrown, so she assumed the airport was closed or maybe even abandoned. Even the grass runway hadn't been mowed in quite some time, and she doubted a plane could land there safely. All the buildings were in disrepair, and she didn't see any signs of life around any of them. In front of the hangar there was a long rectangular pole barn for aircraft, yet only two of the slots actually had planes parked in them. Grass and weeds had grown up around the planes, as if no one had flown either one in months or even years. She pulled around behind the first plane, hoping that the small structure would shield her car from the road and not attract unwanted visitors. She would have her hands full with the man she was already expecting.

She parked, then looked around her carefully, hoping that there was no one working in the hangar who would challenge her. Everything looked abandoned, yet she didn't want to take any unnecessary chances. Acres of pine trees surrounded the airport, and someone could have easily been hiding in the woods without her knowledge. She wondered fleetingly where Dominic and Jake were hidden, but she didn't see any sign of them, nor did she expect to. She glanced around cautiously once again, then got out and grabbed the small cooler out of the trunk and headed toward the hangar. Martin would probably appear soon enough, pulling in with his car as soon as she was out of range to see or hear him. The faster she could get her hands on that disk, the better.

SIXTEEN

The large hangar doors that slid open to get the planes in and out were rusted and bent and didn't quite close, even though the handles were chained and padlocked together. Jessica probably could have squeezed herself through the small opening if she'd had to, but there was another regular sized door to the left and she headed for that, hoping it wasn't locked.

Her heart was pounding with each step she took and her mouth felt dry. Even though she had chosen to do this, fear still coursed within her. The doorknob turned easily in her hand, and she went into the building, unaware of the silver sedan that was slowly pulling around the hangar out of her line of sight.

The door she'd opened led straight into the hangar, yet once inside it was hard to see. The only light coming into the building was from the partial opening between the large hangar doors. She looked for a light switch, found one near the door and flicked it on. The floor of the hangar had at one time been a concrete slab, but parts of it were crumbled and weeds were growing abundantly along the cracks despite the lack of sunshine.

The light also illuminated two small planes that were in the middle of the hangar. The first was a red and white Cessna that had obviously been parked there for some time. Mold grew over most of the windows, and green algae covered a large part of the wings. It also had a broken window, and the inside of the plane was just as filthy as the outside.

She walked cautiously over to the other plane, keeping her eyes open for anyone else that might enter the hangar. This one was a blue-and-white Grumman Cougar, also covered with algae and mold, but apparently in slightly better condition than the Cessna. It sported a broken prop and flat tires, but the inside of the plane was on the cleaner side.

She saw movement out of the corner of her eye near one of the Grumman's wings, and a stab of fear went down her spine. She took a step closer, trying to get a better view. "Is anybody there?" She took another step, then flinched involuntarily when she saw an enormous black banana spider moving on its web. Relief washed over her. She had never liked spiders, but they were far better than finding a hit man trying to kill her. Logically, she knew Martin probably wouldn't approach her until she had the disk in hand, but that knowledge did nothing to slow her speeding pulse. She turned away from the planes and headed back toward the rear of the building.

The heat in the hangar was stifling, and sweat was already trickling down her back, even though she'd only been in the building for a few minutes. She wiped her brow, then started walking toward the back of the building. She went to the door marked "office" and was instantly relieved when the knob also turned easily in her hand, just as Michael had said.

She walked into the room and flipped on the office light. A small cot was set up in the back, and there was also a desk with papers strewn about and a large filing cabinet. A rusty oscillating fan and a couple of novels were on top of a small refrigerator, and she breathed a sigh of relief when she heard the low hum from the motor. Although the refrigerator didn't look like much, she was met with deliciously cool air when she opened the door, and she smiled with relief. There were several cans of soda pop in the front, but tucked into the corner was a brown grocery bag wrapped tightly with packing tape. She pulled at the tape and opened the bag. Inside were two small boxes filled with medicine vials and a mini-CD in a plastic case. She slipped the CD into her pocket, then closed the bag back up and put it in her cooler with the cold packs she had brought carefully rearranged around it. All she had to do now was hand over the evidence to Dominic and a large part of Michael's problems would be over.

"Thanks. That will make it much easier for me to carry."

Jessica jumped at the voice, completely surprised that someone had approached her from behind without her knowing it. She spun her head around and saw a brawny man in shorts and a blue polo shirt not ten feet behind her. He was wearing sunglasses that concealed his eyes and a dark baseball cap, but Jessica recognized him as the man in the picture that Dominic had showed her before they had arrested Michael at the restaurant. He had a grim expression on his face that made him look sinister and dangerous. He was also pointing a pistol right at her chest.

"Who are you?" she asked, a sliver of fear in her voice. She already knew the answer, but she was scared, and the words just popped out of her mouth.

"I'm the one who's going to take that disk away from you. Now put that cooler on the floor and back away from it."

Jessica didn't move. "You work for Coastal, don't you?"

The man's expression darkened. Clearly he had no patience for questions. He took a menacing step toward her, then another. "Do as I say, and do it now." He hadn't raised his voice, but the implicit threat was obvious.

She did as she was told, and once she had backed away, he picked up the cooler and motioned toward her body with the gun.

"Now get that disk out of your pocket and put it on the floor in front of you. Nice and easy, you hear me?"

She fleetingly considered trying to push by him when he reached for the disk. He must have read that in her expression, because he straightened his arm so that the gun was only a few inches from her forehead, and she found herself staring into the barrel.

"Do it, and I'll shoot you right here, right now. Do you hear me?"

"I hear you," she said quietly. The room was small, and there was no way she could make it out the door past him anyway. She nodded and followed his directions, then took a few steps back.

Martin reached forward and got the disk, then held it up and examined it. Satisfied, he put it in the cooler with the medicine and then shut the lid with a snap. "Now out. Slowly."

Her legs were trembling as she left the small office, and her heartbeat felt like it would leap out of her chest when she heard scraping noises behind her. She dared a look at the man and saw him grabbing a shovel leaning up against the wall. He noticed her look and threw the shovel toward her. It landed noisily on the concrete by her feet. "Pick that up, and remember, if you try anything, my next bullet will go in your brain."

She dared another question. "You've got the disk and the medicine. What more do you want?"

"Well, lady, I want to keep making loads of money at Coastal, and that's not going to happen as long as you're around. You know way too much. I've got the same problem with your brother, so I'm gonna have to kill him, too, but don't worry. I'll be sure to make his death look like an accident, so no one will be asking any questions. Sorry I can't say the same for yours. Now head outside. Go."

Jessica hesitated, not sure if Martin had said enough to really implicate himself or not. Were threats enough? Should she call in the marshals now or try to get him to say a little more? She said a small prayer for wisdom and strength and left the hangar as the man followed closely behind her, his gun pointed at her spine.

"Turn right," Martin said roughly.

She followed his directions and ended up going behind the back of the hangar where they were out of sight from the road. He motioned generally toward the ground with his gun.

"Dig, and don't stop until I tell you to."

His command startled her. "What?"

"I said, *dig*." His voice brooked no room for argument, and he leveled the pistol at her heart.

Jessica looked around nervously. "Where?"

Martin again motioned with the pistol, this time with exasperation as he rolled his eyes. "Right by your feet, Blake. Now get going before I lose my patience completely."

The man's expression was cold and lethal, and Jessica could tell that if she didn't do exactly what he said, he'd shoot her right then. Yes, the marshals would sweep in and arrest him immediately—but she'd still be dead. She started digging. Her heart was already beating out of her chest, but now her hands started trembling uncontrollably, and she had trouble even holding onto the shovel. The reason for the task wasn't lost on her. She was digging her own grave. She saw it in the man's expression and the small curve of his lips. This man was enjoying her fear and was looking forward to taking her life. He was even dragging out the situation so that he could take pleasure in his power and control.

"Freeze!" The command came from behind her, and Jessica's head snapped to see the speaker, even though she recognized the voice. Dominic stood about twenty feet away near the tree line, and was pointing a 9 mm handgun at her captor. He was wearing a bulletproof vest that had U.S. Marshal stamped across it in large yellow letters, and his expression was implacable.

"U.S. Marshal," Jake said loudly, coming from the opposite direction, his gun also drawn and pointed at Martin. Jessica breathed a sigh of relief. The cavalry had arrived and just in time. She didn't think Martin would have waited too much longer before shooting her and throwing her body into the newly dug hole.

Martin grimaced, but he stood motionless, not three feet behind Jessica who was holding the shovel in mid air, still filled with dirt. He inched slowly to the left, keeping Jessica between himself and Dominic. "You're not going to fire," he said defiantly, "because if you do, I *will* shoot the woman. Her blood will be on your hands. Put your guns down and back away, then let me take the cooler and be on my way. That's the only way I'll let the woman live."

Dominic shook his head. "You're the one who needs to put the gun down. Slowly. You're surrounded, and you will not escape. If you shoot her, you'll go to prison for murder. We'll add that to your other charges, and a few months from now, you'll be sitting on death row, trying to figure out what you want to eat for your last meal."

"What's another murder charge?" Martin asked, his voice mocking. He glanced around him, then gave a wicked smile. "I see only two," he sneered, his gun still pointed directly at Jessica, "and I'm an excellent marksman. Even if you get me, and that's a big if, I'll get the girl and at least one of you in the bargain. I'll give you five seconds to put your gun down. Otherwise, I'll kill the woman."

"And I'll kill this marshal," a new voice said fiercely. Chris Riggs suddenly emerged from the left near the door with his hands on his head in a show of surrender. He had obviously been disarmed, and his face was covered with fury and frustration. A man was just a few steps behind him, pointing a wicked-looking Glock at Chris's head. Jessica recognized him as Chuck Holiday—Dominic had showed her a picture. His expression brooked no room for argument, and his eyes were rimmed in red and had a crazed glower to them. "Now put your guns down like the man said."

SEVENTEEN

Fear slammed into Dominic's heart when he saw Chris come around the building with a gun to his head, and he knew down deep that the odds of no one getting hurt in this situation were zero to none. His eyes went to Jake's, and he saw the same concern mirrored back at him. Both Martin and Holiday were extremely dangerous men with very little to lose.

He looked back at Martin, and could tell by the man's body language that his promise to kill Jessica was no idle threat. The man would shoot her at point-blank range and not think twice about it. Martin knew his options had disappeared now that law enforcement had caught up to him, and the threat of extra murder charges at this point meant nothing. He could never return to his life at Coastal after being caught in this situation with the disk at his feet. His only hope was to kill Jessica and the marshals and then try to get away before anyone else discovered the murders. It made him a very dangerous adversary.

Dominic glanced over at Holiday, who was also in a desperate situation. The man had thrown away his career and was headed for prison as soon as the whistle was publicly blown on his deceitfulness. He was in too deep to ever go back, and he had to realize that Jake had documented everything they suspected about his involvement with Coastal. His only real option was to try to kill the marshals who knew about his traitorous behavior and escape before the story broke and the rest of the task force discovered what he had done.

Dominic, however, couldn't let Jessica die. She meant too much to him. Law enforcement personnel were trained to handle themselves in dangerous situations like this one and accept the risks, but Jessica was a civilian and an innocent one at that. Besides that, he loved her. He had only known her for a few days, but he had never felt so close to a woman in his entire life. She was a joy to be around, even when she was throwing drawers at his head or thumping him on the chest. Her zeal and zest for life were infectious, and she made him happy just by being in the same room with him, even when she was crying her eyes out. There was no doubt about it. Jessica Blake was beautiful, inside and out, and she had woven herself into his heart.

He gripped his weapon as emotion swept through him. He was filled with recrimination for letting her participate in this bust in the first place. How could he have agreed to this crazy scheme? He probably would have had to handcuff her to the furniture again to keep her from participating, but at least then she wouldn't be here right now with Martin's gun pointing at her.

His only concern now was keeping her safe. No matter what else happened, she had to live through this.

She just had to. He inched to the left, hoping to get a clearer shot at Martin, glancing at Jake as he did so and motioning toward Holiday with his eyes. If Jake could take out Holiday, Dominic could get Martin before Jessica got hurt.

"You're not listening, Dominic," Holiday said tightly, his voice lethal. "Stop right where you are and slowly put down your weapon. We don't want to kill you, and you don't want to be dead." He paused for emphasis. "There's only one way for this to end without someone dying. You and Jake put your guns down and back away. We'll take the woman with us to make sure you don't try anything stupid, and after we're away safely, we'll let her go."

Before Dominic or Jake could decide their next move, Jessica turned quickly and threw a shovelful of dirt at Jeff Martin's face. Martin took a step backward and fired, and a mere second later, a second shot went off. Martin staggered back as a red circle started to spread slowly across his upper chest. He looked down at the blood, a surprised look in his eyes, then dropped the gun and crumpled forward, his face in the dirt.

At the same instant that the gunfire erupted, Chris elbowed Holiday hard in the stomach, then turned and hit him in the face with an uppercut. A blow from Chris's foot knocked the gun away, and it landed in the grass a few feet away. Holiday staggered but revived quickly and tackled Chris. Both men went down, wrestling to reach the gun first.

"Freeze!" Jake ordered, pointing his weapon at Holiday. He bent down and picked up the fallen gun himself, his own weapon never wavering. Within seconds Chris pulled away from Holiday's grasp, spun him around and slapped his handcuffs on the traitor's wrists.

Dominic raced forward and pulled Jessica into his arms from where she had also fallen to the ground. She had been smart to get down out of the line of fire, and he was anxious to praise her for her quick thinking. But she didn't answer when he called her name, and when he reached out to touch her, his hand came away wet with blood. His body tensed so tightly at the sight that he could barely breathe. He looked quickly at Jessica's face and saw that her eyes were full of pain, and her own breathing was ragged and short.

"I'm sorry, Dominic," she whispered, her voice straining. "Maybe I shouldn't have thrown that dirt at him. I just didn't know what else to do."

Dominic pushed a button on his radio and quickly ordered an ambulance, then turned his full attention back to Jessica. His heart was beating so hard that it felt as if it would come right through his chest. She couldn't die! He loved her with everything inside of him. He didn't want to think about what his life would be like without her. In fact, the very idea seemed inconceivable. She had to live. That was all there was to it. She just had to.

"Shh," he whispered softly, trying to keep his voice calm so he wouldn't scare her even more. "Help is coming." He pulled back enough of her shirt to see the small entrance wound on her side, then moved her slightly to find the exit wound. Both holes were seeping blood. He'd originally thought that Martin's shot had gone wild, but the man hadn't missed his target after all. With an economy of motion Dominic pulled out a medical pad from one of the compartments on his belt, unwrapped it and pressed it to the exit wound, trying to staunch the flow of blood.

"I wanted you to know," she whispered again, "that I…" She started coughing, and blood sputtered out of her mouth and painted her chin and neck with bright red droplets.

Dominic felt his heart constrict as he watched her struggling to breathe and losing so much blood at the same time. He knew instinctively that her wounds were deadly serious, and a wave of dread like he had never felt before swept over him from head to toe. He forced himself to focus, then tried to soothe her with his words. She needed him to be strong for her, and he wouldn't let her down. "Don't talk, sweetheart. Help is coming. Do you hear me? Help is coming." He glanced over at Jake, who was now checking on Martin.

"She's hit," Dominic said, his voice breaking. "Bring me a pad from your belt, will you?"

Jake rushed to his side and pulled out another medical pad from his own belt so Dominic could hold it to the entrance wound as well. "Here you go. How bad is it?"

"Looks like it got her lung. She's having trouble breathing."

"Martin's still alive," Jake stated, then spoke into his radio, updating the dispatcher of their situation. When he finished, he turned back to Dominic and put his hand on his shoulder. "Ambulance will be here in ten," he said quietly. "I'll have Chris go wait by the road and direct them over here. Keep pressure on those wounds."

"The disk…"

Jessica coughed some more, and Dominic put his hands on both sides of her face so that their eyes met. His expression was fierce. "Forget the disk! Don't die! Do you hear me? Don't die! You hang in there." She coughed and sputtered, but Dominic kept speaking, his eyes locked with hers, willing her to fight. "Stay with me, Jessica. You're strong. You can do this. Don't give up. Do you hear me? Help is coming."

Jessica reached up to touch the tears running down Dominic's face, but she couldn't seem to answer him. She was struggling too much to breathe, and the words just wouldn't come. Dominic tried to maintain eye contact, but slowly her eyes lost their focus, and he could tell that he was losing her.

"Jessica!" Dominic yelled, seeing the light go from her eyes and her body go slack. He felt frantically for a pulse on her neck, but he was shaking so badly he couldn't find it. Jake moved his hand to help him, but Dominic batted it away, oblivious to the blood that had coated his skin. "She can't die. She can't. She's going to live through this."

He repositioned his fingers, then took a deep breath as he found the pulse. She had lost consciousness, but her heart was still beating. "Thank God. She's still alive." He put his cheek next to her lips to verify that she was still breathing. Her breath was faint, but it was there. He held her closely, pressing the pads to her wounds and praying fervently for her life until the ambulance arrived a few minutes later, and the emergency personnel pried her from his arms.

The emergency technicians quickly took control of the situation. They moved rapidly to provide oxygen, control the bleeding and get her condition stabilized all at once. Dominic still knelt on the ground, frozen, as he watched them work. Jessica's blood covered his shirt, arms and hands and had soaked into the ground around him, but he barely seemed to notice it. He stared at the tree line, but all he could see was the pain radiating in her soft blue eyes as she had lost consciousness.

Jake put his hand on Dominic's shoulder in a motion of comfort, and Dominic stood slowly. "Come on, Deputy."

"I think the bullet got her lung," Dominic repeated softly.

"I think you're right," Jake agreed, "but they'll take good care of her. Why don't you ride in the ambulance with her to the hospital? Chris and I will take care of the scene, then meet you there when we're finished. I'll bring the laptop over and you can write up your report while she's in surgery. It'll give you something to do."

Dominic nodded, his expression showing his appreciation. He pulled the car keys out of his pocket and handed them to Jake. "Thanks." One of the EMTs motioned for Dominic to come, and he quickly jumped in the ambulance right before the other EMT shut the door and latched it firmly. A few moments later, the ambulance pulled away, the lights and sirens blazing.

Dominic settled in by Jessica's side, his heart in his

throat as he gently held her hand and caressed her palm with his thumb. He couldn't ever remember praying harder than he was praying right now.

EIGHTEEN

"The bullet punctured the lower lobe of her left lung," the doctor said in a matter-of-fact tone. He had a small blue notebook with him, and he actually drew a diagram of some lungs and ribs to point out where Jessica had sustained her injuries so Dominic could better understand what had happened.

"We were able to stop the bleeding and reinflate it, but she lost a lot of blood, and has a couple of broken ribs." The man wiped some sweat off his brow with a small towel and continued. "Half an inch to the right, and she probably would have bled to death internally. Half an inch to the left, and she would have been paralyzed. Someone was watching out for her out there, that's for sure." He patted Dominic on the back, trying to reassure him. "She's out of danger now, and her vital signs are strong, but it will be a slow recovery. In fact, it will probably be several weeks before she's back to one hundred percent."

Dominic nodded, sweet relief flowing through him. She would live. He had felt so powerless after he'd discovered that Martin's bullet had knocked her to the ground. As a result, he had replayed the scene at the airport over and over again in his mind, condemning himself for what he could have or should have done differently. Despite his guilt and frustration, however, he had grasped the important part of the doctor's news. Jessica was alive, and God was watching out for her. "Can I see her?"

The doctor checked his watch. "In about fifteen minutes. They're moving her up to ICU on the third floor. Don't be alarmed if she is still unconscious for a while. She's on some heavy medication and will be in a lot of pain when she wakes up."

Dominic nodded as he glanced at his own watch to check the time. Even if he couldn't speak to her, he wanted to see with his own eyes that she had survived the surgery. It wasn't that he didn't believe the doctor; he just needed some new images of her in his mind to replace the bloody scene from the airport. "Thanks for everything, Doc." He shook hands with the surgeon and watched him leave, then turned to see Jake who was just closing his cell phone after a lengthy conversation.

Jake raised an eyebrow. "Good news?"

"Yeah," Dominic answered tightly. "The doctor said she'll pull through, she just has a few weeks of recovery ahead of her. She has a collapsed lung and a few broken ribs. They're moving her to ICU." He shifted impatiently. All he really wanted to do was go sit by Jessica's side, but he still had a duty to perform. "What did you find out?"

"Martin's going to live, although he's in critical condition. He survived the surgery and the prognosis is good.

We've got a guard on him, but he's not going anywhere anytime soon. When he's stable enough to travel, they'll ship him over to the prison's medical ward."

Dominic soaked in the information, then ran his hands through his hair. In some ways, it was easier to focus on the case against Coastal than it was to think about Jessica lying in a hospital bed three flights up. "Any way we can tie the two together? You know the order to kill came from Ross Kelley himself."

"We'll see once he regains consciousness. Of course, Kelley will probably say that Martin took matters into his own hands when he thought the counterfeiting scheme was in danger. But who knows? Maybe we can get Martin to testify against Kelley, too."

"Well, at least we've got Martin for the attempted murder and tampering with evidence. With that and Michael's testimony, he'll be going away for a good long time. What did the disk show?"

"Everything we hoped. The documents tied in Kelley and Martin, and now we've got them both for forgery, too, because of all the fake documents they used to try to cover up their scheme. The two boxes of medicine we recovered with the disk were Neupogen, just as we thought. Neither box appeared to have been tampered with, but they're still at the lab."

"What about Holiday?"

Jake was quiet for a moment, clearly affected by the man's treachery. "Refusing to talk, but we've got him dead to rights. It'll be harder to prove that he was involved with Levine's death, but I've got clear recordings of him contacting Martin and telling him about

Jessica's whereabouts, not to mention all of the other electronic evidence we have against him. Of course, there's also everything that happened at the airport. Internal Affairs has already swooped in and taken over the case."

"Did the district attorney already get the warrants issued against Kelley?"

Jake nodded. "Yep. The marshals in Atlanta are on the way over right now to execute them. He should be under arrest and enjoying his new living quarters at the jail within the hour."

"That's good to hear," Dominic stated, clearly distracted by his worry for Jessica. "Look, I'm going to go up and make sure Jessica gets settled in."

Jake nodded again, understanding painted on his face. "Tell her I'm praying for her."

Dominic gave him a grateful smile. "Absolutely. Thanks." He turned and walked down the hall until he came to the elevators, but when none arrived after several minutes of pressing the call button, he took the stairs instead and made his way up to the third floor. He located the nurse's station, then paced a few minutes while he waited impatiently for the nurse to give him permission to enter Jessica's room. Finally, the nurse beckoned him with her finger and he followed her back through the ICU doors and into a room on the right behind a glass partition.

Despite the doctor telling him about her condition, seeing Jessica in the hospital's ICU setting was still a shock. Her skin was pale and tubes wove in and out around her body, machines humming and clicking, making a symphony of background noises. He came to her side and reached for her hand, then gave it a gentle squeeze and caressed it with his thumb.

He looked down at their entwined fingers, his tanned and long, hers small and dainty against his skin, and marveled at the rightness of it. She was so beautiful to him, even in her present condition. He swallowed the lump in his throat, wanting desperately to see her open her eyes and give him her smile. At this point, he'd even be happy if she threw another drawer at him, if only she would wake up so he could see for himself that she was going to be okay. He closed his eyes and said another prayer, then brushed his free hand gently against her cheek.

"Jessica, you have to be strong. God will help you." He paused and closed his eyes, gathering his own strength. "I'm so sorry you got hurt. When I realized you had been hit, my whole world turned upside down." He squeezed her hand again, then gently cupped her face in his hands. Now, after everything that had happened, he was finally able to express the words that were in his heart, even if she wasn't awake to hear them. "I love you, Jessica Blake." He bent over and gave her a kiss on her forehead, thanking God over and over again for sparing her life.

It was a few hours later when the nurse touched Dominic lightly on the shoulder. "Sir? Sir?"

Dominic stirred. He was way too big to be sleeping on these uncomfortable waiting room chairs, but he hadn't wanted to leave the hospital in case Jessica regained consciousness sometime during the night. He had gone home to change clothes and clean up, but had returned soon after, only to find there was no change in her condition. He wiped the sleep out of his eyes and stretched to work the kinks out of his muscles. "Is she awake?"

"Yes, for about ten minutes now. She's in a lot of pain, but I think you can have a few minutes with her if you keep it short."

"You bet," Dominic promised. He stood quickly, anxious to see her, and followed the nurse into the intensive care unit.

He was surprised to see that she even looked worse now than she had before. Her skin was still pale, but this time her eyes had dark circles under them from the pain and fatigue. At least her eyes were open, though. It tore at his heart that she had to endure such suffering, but he certainly wasn't going to complain about finally seeing those beautiful blue eyes again. He wouldn't complain about seeing them every day, for the rest of his life.

Jessica's entire body seemed to hurt, and exhaustion made it hard for her to think. Despite the pain, however, she attempted to give Dominic a smile when he approached her bed. His dark gray eyes were hard to read, especially in her weakened condition, but she figured he was probably still pretty angry about her throwing the dirt at Martin. She couldn't remember much that had happened after that, but she had ended up in the hospital, so the whole affair couldn't have ended well. She wondered fleetingly if anyone else had gotten hurt. She sure hoped not.

"How are you, Jessica?" Dominic asked quietly, his voice laced with worry.

"I hurt," she answered softly. As if to emphasize her words a pain shot through her wound, and she grimaced. With every breath, it felt as if her entire chest was on fire.

Dominic reached for her hand and squeezed it gently. "I know. I'm so sorry this happened to you. It's all my fault."

His words surprised her. "Your fault? What are you talking about?"

He shook his head. "I should never have let you go to that airport. It was the worst decision I've ever made."

"Let me? Look, Marshal, I didn't give you a lot of choice. If this is anybody's fault, it's mine. I know I probably shouldn't have thrown that dirt at Martin, but I wanted to distract him…." She stopped on a sob, suddenly overcome by pain and emotion, and he brushed the hair out of her eyes and tenderly wiped the tears away.

"Shhh. It's okay," he said gently. "It's over now."

"But I made such big mistakes…."

Dominic silenced her with a warm kiss on her lips, then moved slightly and kissed her forehead. "What are you talking about? Because of you, we've got Martin and Holiday both in custody. Even Ross Kelley has been arrested. You were incredibly brave, by the way. You did an amazing job. I'm just so sorry that you got hurt in the process."

Jessica watched him lean back and smile at her, but she was too stunned to smile back. Had he just kissed her? Twice? Why wasn't he furious with her? She looked at him carefully and noticed the tired lines around his eyes and haggard expression, not to mention his rumpled clothes and day's growth of beard on his face. Maybe he was just too exhausted right now to tell her how much she had disappointed him by her actions at the airport. But that didn't explain the kisses. Had she hallucinated those?

"How long have you been here?"

Dominic shrugged. "Long enough to know those hospital chairs out there in the waiting room are made for smaller people, and they don't make good beds."

She laughed, then grimaced as another pain gripped her chest. It was way too early to be finding anything humorous at this point. She squeezed his hand tightly, then gradually loosened her grip as the pain subsided. Finally, she met his eyes again. "What happened to the man who shot me? I asked before, but no one would tell me."

"He's a few floors away in critical condition." Dominic answered. "He's under guard, so he won't be going anywhere but to prison once he recovers. You don't have to worry about him bothering you ever again."

Jessica digested that information and jumped to the logical conclusion. "Did you shoot him?"

"Yes, I did."

She could tell from his expression that he took firing his weapon at another human being very seriously, but it had been necessary, and she understood that.

"How's Michael doing?"

"He's fine, though he's worried about you. Whitney

brought him by earlier but you were sleeping. He'll have to stay in custody until all of this gets sorted out."

She closed her eyes briefly, then pushed on.

"So what about the leak? You said he was in custody, too, right?"

"Yeah, that's right. When you threw the dirt, it caused enough of a distraction that Chris was able to get the gun away from him without any more shots being fired."

"What about the disk?"

"Safe and in the hands of the FBI and the prosecutor. It had everything on it that we hoped. The Coastal CEO who ordered the hits and ran the whole counterfeiting scheme is also in custody. I imagine Kelley is enjoying his first jailhouse breakfast this morning as we speak."

Jessica closed her eyes for a moment. "I'm so glad. I didn't want Coastal to keep on counterfeiting medicine. I was afraid you couldn't stop them without that disk, even if Michael did testify."

Dominic ran his fingers down her cheek. "Don't worry. We've got ample proof now about the whole situation. Coastal's counterfeiting days are over, once and for all."

Jessica gave a small smile, relief painted on her face. Her body shuddered as if a giant weight had been removed from her shoulders. "Oh, Dominic, that's really good to hear. I was so afraid that Michael was lost forever, but now that he told you the truth about the disk, it seems like he might be on the right track again. It won't be easy for him to testify against Kelley, but it's the right thing to do. I really believe that." She suddenly grimaced as another pain shot through her wound. An uncomfortable drainage tube still protruded from her chest, and the nurse had told her that it would probably have to remain there for another day or two until they knew for sure that the lung was properly reinflated. It didn't hurt half as much as her ribs did, though, and every breath reminded her of what had transpired during the last twenty-four hours.

She shifted and gritted her teeth, trying to get the pain to subside. A few moments later the throbbing lessened a bit and she closed her eyes, gathering her strength. When she opened them again she noticed Dominic watching her carefully, and she gazed at him, trying to read his expression. What she saw made her catch her breath all over again. She had never seen such tenderness or angst displayed so vividly. The fact that those emotions were directed at her made her heart soar, despite her injuries.

Dominic leaned over and lifted her hand gently to his lips, then moved his lips to hers and seemed to savor the softness of them. "You know, that was the first time you called me Dominic instead of Marshal. I like that." He closed his eyes for a moment, then opened them again. "I was so worried about you being involved in the arrest, and then when I saw you again out at the airport, I realized I couldn't go on without you in my life. When you got shot, my whole world shattered." He locked eyes with her as if looking deep into her soul through those clear blue depths. "I love you, Jessica."

Jessica caught her breath, searching his eyes. She saw only truth reflected there, but his words were hard to believe. "Are you sure? I mean, you seemed like you wanted to distance yourself away from me...."

Dominic shook his head, trying to convince her. "You're right, I did—but that was because I was afraid I couldn't love you and do my job well at the same time. Now, it just doesn't matter. I'll get reassigned or do whatever I need to to make sure you're safe." Tears had started trickling down her cheek, and he gently wiped them away with his thumb. "You're in my heart now, Jessica, and I'm warning you, I'm never going to let you go. That's a promise." He ran his thumb gently over her bottom lip, then kissed her softly. "I love you."

Instead of drying her tears, his words caused them to flow even more freely. "Oh, Dominic." She gripped his hand, happiness shining in her eyes. "I love you, too." She grimaced then as pain swept through her, and Dominic stood and brushed the hair away from her face in a gesture of love.

The nurse came in and tapped him on the shoulder, and he nodded in response, then turned back to Jessica. He smiled at her, his eyes dancing. "Rest now. I'll come back later after you've had a chance to sleep a little more."

She nodded but didn't want to release his hand. The nurse adjusted a dial, and she felt a numbness sweep over her. There was still a lot of uncertainty in her future, but she knew now that both God and Dominic would be there with her on her road to recovery. A smile touched her lips as she drifted off to sleep, her heart finally at peace.

EPILOGUE

Dominic took another piece of fried chicken out of the picnic basket, then leaned back against the blanket and watched as Jessica pushed her little niece in the swing. Julia was alternating between giggling and shrieking with joy as Jessica made the swing move in rhythm to a rhyming song she was singing. A sense of peace invaded Dominic's heart as he watched the two, and his eyes fixed on Jessica. She was stunning, even in her simple jeans and dark blue sweater, and her face glowed with health and happiness. It had been eight months since she had been shot, and she had healed up quite nicely. They had spent a huge amount of time together as she had recovered, and his love for her had grown even deeper with each passing day.

He looked over at her brother Michael who was standing with Sandy, his fiancée, by the other end of the swing. They were enjoying their conversation together yet still keeping a watchful eye on their daughter. Both Michael and Sandy had recently started attending a Bible study at their church. Although neither had given their lives to the Lord yet, they were both at least interested in what Dominic and Jessica had discovered and were trying to learn more about God and their faith.

Sandy had pled *nolo contendre* to receiving stolen property in exchange for a sentence of two hundred community service hours. She had spent the bulk of that time volunteering at the hospital in the children's ward. Michael had been able to find a decent job with a local distribution company and was working hard to provide for his tiny family. He had been also able to arrange an excellent plea bargain with the district attorney in exchange for his testimony against Coastal, yet in the end, he hadn't even needed to testify. Ross Kelley had worked out his own plea bargain by agreeing to testify against some of his contacts in the business, and he was now serving twenty to twenty-five years in a federal penitentiary. Jeff Martin had survived the shooting with some loss of motion in his right arm but had otherwise recovered fully. Both he and Chuck Holiday were now serving a life sentence in a maximum security federal prison.

Dominic glanced over at his two brothers, Alex and Ryan, who were a short distance away tossing a baseball back and forth. They had both teased him quite a bit since he was the first of the three to be involved in a serious dating relationship, but they had welcomed Jessica into the family with open arms. Alex had even agreed to represent Sandy and Michael in their fight to get Julia's medicine covered by Medicaid, and in the meantime, Ryan had found a private organization to help cover the costs so the little girl's life wouldn't be in danger.

Jessica let Michael take over at the swing and walked over to sit next to Dominic on the blanket. She opened the picnic basket and reached for an apple. "How's the chicken?"

"Marvelous," Dominic answered with a smile. It was time. A wave of nervousness swept up his spine, yet he tapped it down as he pulled the small box out of his pocket. "Can I have everyone's attention, please?" He gestured to his brothers and Michael and Sandy, urging them over near the blanket. Sandy got Julia out of the swing, and the group slowly converged around Dominic and Jessica. Jessica's face showed her confusion as Dominic touched her cheek gently and he pulled her to her feet.

"What's up, little brother?" Alex asked playfully, still tossing the ball into his mitt.

"I wanted you all to be a part of this." He locked eyes with Jessica and was bolstered by the love he saw reflected back at him. He knew the last eight months had been an incredible journey for her as well, and not just physically as her wounds had healed. As their relationship had grown and bloomed day by day, he had also seen her relationship with the Lord grow and strengthen. As he looked at her now, his heart felt so full it felt as if it would burst at any moment. He opened the box, revealing the ring, and placed it in her hand, then grasped her other hand and went down on one knee. "Jessica Blake, would you please do me the honor of marrying me?"

Jessica gasped and covered her mouth with her hand. Pure joy radiated from her face, even as tears of happiness filled her eyes. "Oh, yes! Dominic, I love you so much!"

The group clapped and whistled as Dominic stood and took Jessica into his arms. He kissed her gently as a sense of excitement and contentment filled his heart. He didn't know what tomorrow would bring, but he knew that he, Jessica and God would face it together, and he would love and protect her for the rest of their lives.

* * * * *

Dear Reader,

I have always been a strong person, and unfortunately, when adversity comes my way, my first response is usually "I can handle this by myself," instead of "God and I can handle this together." My husband and I have eight children, five of whom we adopted. One is a special-needs child who has severe mental disabilities as well as a blood disease and shortened anticipated lifespan. Through this precious child, God is teaching me that I am not in control at all, but that He is in control. He has also proven Himself faithful and given me the strength to love and care for my son on the good days as well as the bad. In my weakness, God is strong!

I wish that I could say that I have learned my lesson, and I always turn to God first when problems arise, but alas, I am a work in progress! I do know that when difficulties come my way, I have two choices; I can either get bitter or better. My prayer is that you will also turn to God for strength, and let God carry you through the rough spots in life, remembering that He will never leave you or forsake you. God will not erase the problems in our lives, but He will definitely be there with us so we won't have to handle them alone.

The Lord is my strength and my shield; My heart trusted in Him, and I am helped; Therefore my heart greatly rejoices, And with my song I will praise Him. Psalms 28:7 NKJV

Kathleen Tailer

QUESTIONS FOR DISCUSSION

1. In the beginning, Jessica tries to handle her problems by herself without leaning on God. Have you ever tried to do that in your own life? What was the result?

2. How do you think losing her parents played into Jessica's protectiveness of her brother?

3. Dominic struggles with keeping his job duties and his emotional desires separate. How did this affect his relationship with Jessica?

4. Is emotion what drives your actions in life? Should it?

5. How did Dominic's actions affect his relationship with his coworkers?

6. Jessica didn't trust Dominic to keep her brother safe from harm, and Michael was afraid to trust the marshals. Have you ever trusted someone who let you down?

7. Do you trust God? Why or why not?

8. Michael stole medicine to help his daughter. Have you ever done something you knew was wrong and justified the action? What was the result?

9. Jessica forgave Michael for taking her hostage at the restaurant. Was this important? What could have happened if she hadn't?

10. Kelley and Martin never considered the impact their actions had on the rest of the Coastal workers or on the unsuspecting public. Why is it important to consider the consequences of what we do before we act?

11. As Jessica was recovering from her injuries, what did she and Dominic do to improve their relationship?

12. Do you have a relationship that needs to be mended? What is holding you back? What does God's Word say to do?

13. What does this verse mean to you? "Trust in the Lord with all your heart, and lean not on your own understanding; in all your ways acknowledge Him, and He shall direct your paths." Proverbs 3:5-6 NKJV

14. Out of all the characters in the book, which one needed God the most?

SUSPENSE

TITLES AVAILABLE NEXT MONTH

Available November 9, 2010

LISCNM1010

LARGER-PRINT BOOKS!

**GET 2 FREE
LARGER-PRINT NOVELS
PLUS 2 FREE
MYSTERY GIFTS**

Love Inspired®

SUSPENSE
RIVETING INSPIRATIONAL ROMANCE

Larger-print novels are now available...

LISUSLP10R